ed
st.

STORNOWAY
Isle of Lewis.

Leaves on a Tree

Leaves on a Tree

Edwina Hawker

SCRIPTURE UNION,
130 City Road, London EC1V 2NJ

Printed and bound in Great Britain by
William Clowes (Beccles) Limited, Beccles and London

A story for
   David,
   Jacqueline and
   Sarah

Historical Note

In ancient times there were two kingdoms in the north of England. Bernicia was in the place that we now call Northumbria. Deira was in the place that we now call Yorkshire.

Ethelfrith, king of the Bernicians, married Acca, a princess of the Deirans, and ruled both kingdoms. But Edwin, Acca's brother, fled from Ethelfrith.

In AD 617 Edwin, with the help of Redwald, king of the East Anglians, defeated Ethelfrith and took the kingdom. Ethelfrith's sons were taken for safety to the land of the Scots, which was on the west side of what is now Scotland, together with many of the western isles. The Scots were Christians of the Celtic culture, and the exiled princes and their friends became Christians.

Edwin reigned over the two kingdoms justly, and was overlord to other kingdoms. He married the daughter of the king of Kent. With the queen, to her new home, came the Roman missionary bishop, Paulinus. In 627 Edwin was baptised as a Christian by Paulinus.

In 633 Penda king of Mercia, the area we now call the Midlands, defeated and killed Edwin, in alliance with the British king, Cadwallon.

Places in the Story

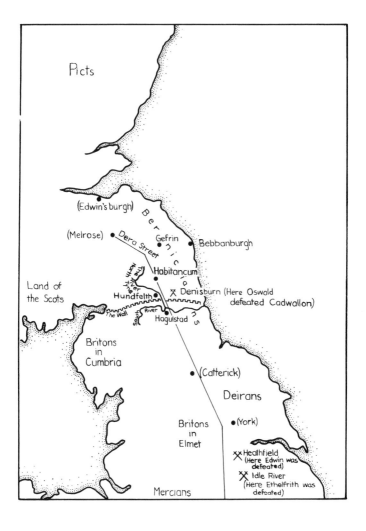

People in the Story

LADY ALDSWITH, mistress of Hundfelth, in Bernicia
EBBA, her daughter
HRETHLA, Ebba's daughter
WIG, the shepherd
GIL, his wife
DUFFA, his son
ORCA, Gil's sister
SIBALD, one of the family of farming people
RENFRITH; Lady Aldswith's youngest son
BEREN, his friend
INGUI, Ebba's husband, who is dead
REDPATH, Lady Aldswith's third son, who is dead
ELFRIC WULFING, a young man from a neighbouring settlement
WULFWINE, his uncle
FREAGIFU, his sister
THURSTAN, a farming man from Deira
MILDRED, his wife
HROSLI, a girl from another settlement
SNIBBA, Hrethla's dog
FEN, the yard dog
BAN, Beren's dog
TRUMHERE, a young man of Bernicia, a pupil of Aidan's
OSWALD, of the Bernician royal family, and AIDAN, a Scots Christian, who were both real people in history

Contents

1 Out on the Wall

'Where's Hrethla?'

'Out with the sheep.'

'If you don't keep that child of yours in order we'll never get her a husband.'

'Don't worry. No-one ever comes near this place anyway.'

Hrethla was out with the sheep. Snibba, the young dog, ran beside her, and the sheep-dog went from side to side, keeping the flock together.

The shepherd's name was Wig. His hair was grey as a fleece; his eyes were amber. He cared a great deal about his flock, and a little about Hrethla and about Gil, his wife, perhaps, and not at all about Duffa, his son, who kept the pigs in the wood.

Wig was taking his sheep to graze beside the Wall. The Wall and the road on its further side cut the wide moor in half from east to west, as far as eye could see. Curving up and down with the hills, it lay like a snake, like a dragon killed long ago and left, stretched out in the open, away from its dark and secret treasure cave. But not even a dragon could be so vast. Hrethla knew that the Wall had been built by Roman soldiers long ago in their wars, before the Engle people came to the land of Britain. It was so huge, and had so many strong towers built along it, even in the few miles that Hrethla knew, that it was hard to think that ordinary men had ever built it.

'Were they giants, Wig?'

'Who, then?'

'The Romans.'

'Not they. You've seen their bones. They're not that big.'

Hrethla had not seen any of their bones. She had found a coin on the Wall and was always looking for another. It was said that when the Romans, who were of course very rich, had gone away, they had buried their golden hoards deep in the earth in many places. If Hrethla could have carried a spade, unobserved, up over the moor from home she would have dug for that treasure and perhaps restored the family fortune.

Wig settled the sheep to graze beside the Wall, and Hrethla climbed up into a look-out tower. She pretended to be a Roman soldier, with a spear as big as a young tree, looking out over the Roman Empire.

Southwards she looked across the road at bare and rolling moor. Westwards the Wall rose and fell, and on the northern side she could make out the reeds and alder trees around the Meres. Looking north the ground fell away to the woods in the valley. Hidden by a ridge of the moor lay Hundfelth, her home, with roofs of broken thatch huddling inside the high grey wooden fence. There her grandmother ruled the farmstead, Lady Aldswith, tall and sharp-featured, usually cross and always bitterly regretting her hard life. Her husband and two of her sons had died in the battle in which Edwin the King had killed his brother-in-law and taken his kingdom. Her next son had died in a scuffle with a neighbour, and the youngest had gone far away, to the land of the Scots, where the young sons of the old King had sought safety. Lady Aldswith had only her daughter left, Ebba, Hrethla's mother, tall like herself, working hard, saying little, and falling, sometimes, into moods of grieving. Hrethla was often angry with her grandmother and often sad with her mother, but when she could she ran out on the moor away from them. Sometimes she went alone, sometimes with Wig, and sometimes with

Orca. Orca was Gil's sister, but she was not wizened and toiling like Gil. She was well-built, with a kind face, and did all the jobs Hrethla found most interesting, like growing the vegetables and searching for herbs on the moor.

These were all the people at Hundfelth and nearly all the people Hrethla knew. Half a mile from the farmstead was a cottage where the family lived that worked the farmland. They were all that was left of the settlement that Hrethla's grandfather had started, back in King Ethelfrith's days.

Turning to the east Hrethla saw the Wall run down to the valley as the river curved south, lose itself and climb again on the other side. How small, how very small, was Hrethla the Roman soldier with her great spear, beside the expanse of sky and moorland, the unseen river in its valley, and the snaky line of the Wall. And how much smaller still the horseman riding up from the east.

'Wig! There's someone coming.'

Wig came up to look, and they went down to the road to find out what the man was doing. He rode alone and fast, but when he came level with them he pulled up.

'Good health,' he called. 'Tell me, fellow, where can I water the horse next?'

'Spring along there.' Wig pointed west. 'Post by the spring, and a brass cup on a chain. Edwin Alla's son had it put.'

'Edwin the King,' said the stranger. 'A ruler to remember.'

'We remember him,' said Wig, with scorn.

'Edwin was brave and just,' said the man. 'You should be ashamed to run him down in front of the boy there.'

Wig snorted. 'That's no boy. She's granddaughter to my Lady Aldswith, and the lady puts all her troubles down to Edwin.'

The horseman looked at Hrethla. He saw her fair hair,

matted and shaggy, the bit of sheepskin knotted over her shoulders, her short dress and bare legs and feet. Hrethla gave him look for look, with steady blue eyes and uplifted chin.

'Ah well,' said the stranger. 'When a man's gone, it's his good fame that lives. The King is dead in battle and all his valiant companions. The army's cut to pieces. There are no fighting men now between you and the Britons, and here am I riding to the land of the Scots to bring the news to the Princes in exile.'

He gathered his reins together. Wig must have looked as if he did not credit the news.

'No man can stand in battle on the day it is decreed that he must fall,' said the man, and rode on.

2 Under the Ash Tree

'Come here, idle bones! Take this and do it by dinner time, or you'll have a beating and no dinner.'

So saying, Lady Aldswith thrust into Hrethla's hands a long thick stick with a great cloud of sheep's wool wound about it, ready combed for spinning.

Hrethla had been about to slip out. She turned and went into the weaving hall instead.

At the front of the weaving hall several looms stood upright at one side and a fire burnt on a grate in the middle of the floor. Ebba stood at one of the looms, working. At the back of the hall were beds, built against the wall, and large wooden boxes, in which clothes, blankets and personal possessions were kept. Hrethla had very few personal possessions. She kept most of them on the shelf over her bed; her Roman coin in an empty pottery jar with a sweet smell left from the face cream Orca had once made, her doll and her spindle, both made for her by Wig out of wood. She collected the spindle and went out.

The weaving hall stood at one side of the Big Hall, which faced the gate. The Big Hall had benches on each side of the door and a high wooden gable, marked with runes. Inside it was cold and musty, with the far end filled with straw. The seats and beds along the wall were not used, and the tables were always stacked, except the one they used in the weaving hall.

Opposite the weaving hall stood the kitchen and the bakehouse, two little square rooms where Lady Aldswith was making bread and Gil was grinding corn on stones for more bread. In front of these was the well, and next to them again was the dairy, then the cow-byre and the stable, with the barn across the yard. Beside the farm buildings there were several one-room living places. One was Wig's and Gil's. Another was Orca's, full of herbs. She usually slept in the weaving hall.

Hrethla picked up a stool from the dairy and went outside. Fen the yard dog growled on his chain, and Snibba came running to her. She put the stool down by the ash tree outside the farmyard gate. At least the weather was still mild. She hated to stay in the weaving hall. As she began to spin, Snibba, regretful, settled at her feet.

It was now late in the year, two months since they had met the messenger on the road, and they had heard nothing more of the outside world. The sun shone low in the sky, for the golden girl who drove the sun from end to end every day had taken it well to the south, as far as she could from the wolves of winter who were always trying to gobble her up.

Wolves did not come close to Hundfelth except in very cold winters. Hrethla had a wolf skin on her bed. It was the winter coat of a huge leader of wolves which her father had killed, ten winters ago, and given to his wife to keep for the baby that was Hrethla. Hrethla thought she ought to be very brave, with a skin like that on her bed.

She was angry when she sat down. If only she had not been caught she would be away across the moor by now. But everybody was working hard. It was only fair that she should work too. Orca was spreading muck on the bean patch round the corner. At the lower end of the field they were ploughing.

The wool that she drew off the distaff and twisted in her fingers made a thread that was sometimes thin and sometimes lumpy. At last it began to run smoothly, winding itself onto her spindle, which dangled about Snibba's ears. Hrethla turned herself into a princess in a story, sitting outside her father's hall, her faithful hound at her feet, spinning a thread of purest gold. But who could tell what would befall this princess? For no man knows what his fate has in store for him. And on the other side of the tree sat the Weird Woman, ancient as time itself, weaving the thread of what-must-be. She wove a thread into the loom; as the pattern fell out so must the course of events; she took her scissors and snipped a thread; so was a man's life cut short. And the tree, of course, was that most wonderful of all trees, the tree that held the world together, and sheltered the destinies of men beneath it. The well of wisdom watered its roots; mystic and mighty it mounted to heaven. Its highest boughs, going straight up, were pillars in the halls of the gods. All manner of creatures in its middle branches found dwelling and sustenance, and every life was bound up with its life. While it flourished, so long should the world endure, but when the Worm that dwelt, gnawing ever at its root, in the depths of Nothingness, should at last destroy it, then would come the end of the world and the loss of every living thing.

Hrethla knew this from Orca's stories, but the princess was her own invention. She was so busy making up the magical adventures of the princess that when a horn blew in the woods, up river, she did not even notice, though it should have warned her that someone was coming. She went on spinning until she felt Snibba stiffen and growl in his throat.

She looked up. A man was coming down towards her. He stopped, several paces away, and said; 'In the Name of Christ, good health. Is this Hundfelth?' Hrethla nodded. 'And what is your name?'

He was tall and well-made, with yellow hair combed smoothly on his shoulders, and a big moustache. His eyes were blue, the colour, Hrethla thought, of the sea, which she had never seen, and the long brooch that pinned his cloak

17

was set with bumpy stones of the same colour. He wore a leather fighting jacket and a big sword, and he looked very fine.

All this Hrethla saw in a moment as she stood up, clutching her stool. She saw too, another man, waiting on the ridge above her, with a couple of horses and a large dog. She said, 'I am Hrethla Ingui's daughter.'

The man's eyes smiled. 'Then fetch your father; he is my friend.'

'He's dead. It's Lady Aldswith you want, my grandmother.' Fen, the yard dog, had begun to bark ferociously. Hrethla could barely hear the man exclaim; 'So you're Ebba's child!' just as Lady Aldswith came to the gate with the others behind her. She took one look, dropped the butcher's knife she was carrying, and threw her arms round the man, kissing him.

'Renfrith, my darling boy! Home at last!' she shouted.

3 Midwinter

At the first pause in the hugging and the kissing, Renfrith said, 'But you must meet Beren, the first of our people that I met when I came to the land of the Scots, and a good friend ever since.'

The man who was holding the horses came down to them. He was dressed like Renfrith but more plainly, he was slighter and his brown hair was mixed with grey. His big brindled dog was called Ban.

'Come along in,' said Lady Aldswith. 'Listen, child. Go and tell them at the cottages that your uncle has come home. Say they can all come up for dinner here to-night.

Hrethla ran down the path through the fields and told Sibald what had happened. He was the youngest of the farming brothers and he was ploughing today. She ran into the woods and found Duffa with the pigs and told him. She ran along the edge of the woods and up to the long, low cottage and its outbuildings. Sibald's two brothers were at work on the new barn they meant to build. She told them, and found the farm wife and told her, and ran back along the track from the cottage all the way to the gate of the farmstead.

It was annoying that in this way she missed hearing how her uncle had come to return, and had to piece the story together from what she could pick up afterwards.

Several messengers had brought to the land of the Scots the news of King Edwin's disastrous defeat, and the princes had made all possible speed to come back and defend their father's kingdom from their uncle's enemies. It took a little while. Many young men of good families had joined the king's sons in their exile, so that each of the princes had a band of fighting men, his own companions, and between them, the makings of a useful army. When they had gathered, they came east, to the royal town of Gefrin in the hills, (which we now call Yeavering) and to Bebbanburgh, (which is Bamburgh now) the fortress that King Ida built. Winter was too far advanced to start a campaign, and while the eldest prince, whom they now called king, mustered support and viewed his lands, with his brothers, their followers had time to see how their own families were faring.

Renfrith and Beren stayed only one night at Hundfelth, but they wasted no time while they were there. When Hrethla came in and put away her distaff and spindle, guessing there would be no more trouble about spinning that day; they were clearing straw out of the Big Hall, having already made the disused stable fit for their horses. Lady Aldswith was preparing a large dinner, and Ebba, smiling, was pouring off her latest brewing of ale.

'Here, Snippet, what's-your-name, Hrethla,' Renfrith called. We're going to the Meres for some reeds. Want to come?'

Hrethla spent a delightful afternoon across the moor. She rode over on the front of her uncle's horse and helped to tie the bundles of reeds which they cut from the shores of the lake while Snibba made friends with the big dog Ban. As they worked, a party of young men came up the burn from the settlement north of the Meres. They were hunting, and the leader of the party was a young man who had evidently just come home, like Renfrith. He greeted them heartily. Renfrith and Beren called him Elfric Wulfing, and also Giltbeard, which Hrethla thought a very suitable nickname. He had blue eyes and crinkly gold hair, with a beard to match and a curly red mouth. She had never seen anyone half as good looking.

20

The young men went on. They stacked the reeds on the horses' backs and walked them home as the light failed.

The tables were set out in the Big Hall. Renfrith took the chief seat, with his mother on one side and his guest on the other. Ebba and Orca, Wig and Gil and the farm people all sat at table, but Hrethla and Duffa had to serve the meat and the ale and stand to eat their dinner at the end of the table with the farm children. Renfrith told them about the land of the Scots.

'They are not as good at farming as we are, but they are wonderful hunters. They gave hospitality to our princes most generously. We hunted with them, we fought with them when the Picts raided their borders, and we learnt from them the truth of the Living God and the faith of the Lord Christ.'

'But that,' said Lady Aldswith, 'is the religion Edwin took up with. And much good it did him! It belongs to the Romans.'

'No,' said Renfrith, 'this faith is for all men. The Scots who were good to us, hold it, and so does our own lord, Oswald Ethelfrith's son, and his brother the king, and the rest of the princes.'

'Well, my dear son, you have come home. And now you will be able to avenge your brother's death on Wulfwine Wulfing.'

Hrethla had so often been told that when her Uncle Renfrith came back he would kill the man who killed her Uncle Redpath, that she half expected him to draw his sword and rush off into the night to do it. However, he sat still.

'Isn't that settled? After all, it was an accident.'

'An accidental killing must be atoned for!' exclaimed Lady Aldswith.

'Of course,' Renfrith agreed. 'But I thought you would have been paid the proper compensation. It must wait, mother mine. We are at war, and we shall have to fight for our land and our lives before we settle accounts with our neighbours.'

'Oh, now Ethelfrith's sons are back in Bernicia we shall soon get the better of those Deirans.'

'It's Cadwallon the Briton and Penda the Mercian king we have to reckon with. They have made an alliance to break the power of whatever king holds Ethelfrith's kingdom. There can be no quarrels between Bernicians and Deirans while that goes on. It's bad enough that bloodshed ever came between Edwin's relations.'

Lady Aldswith did not like this.

'If there is not too much trouble, I shall come back for the Midwinter Feast,' said Renfrith, changing the subjerct. 'May I bring Beren with me? He is a man of Bernicia through and through. He comes from Gefrin and he guarded the young princes when they fled to the land of the Scots. But he has no close family of his own to go to and no land of his own.'

'Any friend of yours is my welcome guest, my son,' said Lady Aldswith grandly.

Hrethla was up early next morning, but not as early as Renfrith and Beren, who had risen from their beds in the Big Hall and were patching the roof with the reeds from the Meres for all they were worth. They also mended the door before riding away that morning, when the Hundfelth people were left to prepare for the best Midwinter Feast they had had for years.

Extra slaughtering, baking, brewing and the collection of firewood went on at a great rate. This was an improvement on spinning, thought Hrethla, especially as the mild weather was gone and every morning brought more frost. There was only time for a little spinning, in the weaving hall, after dinner. Then one evening, Ebba happily filled a bowl with hot water and washed Hrethla's hair. Hrethla was not used to this, and the soap, which was very strong, ran into her eyes. But what happened next was worse. When it was only half dry at the fire, Ebba made her sit on a box and combed her hair through with a big wooden comb. Hrethla set her teeth. She was a fighting man suffering torture at the hands of her enemies. Not a cry escaped her lips. When it was done Ebba looked her up and down.

'I think you've grown out of that dress,' she said.

She rummaged in her box until she found a dress she had worn when she was younger, and tried it on Hrethla. It was too big, but Ebba and Orca turned it up and took it in. The underdress was of pale creamy wool, and the overdress was pale brown with dark brown leaves all over it, woven in. Hrethla had never had anything so fine on her back before, and she felt very grown up when she dressed in it on the morning of the Midwinter Feast.

Everything was ready. Wig had killed a pig the day before, so that they should have fresh meat, and Sibald had actually taken time off to go hunting and brought in some venison. Orca had saved honey from the brewing of mead and made cakes and sweets with white of egg and butter. The children liked these better than anything. Hrethla and Duffa had brought up sprays of holly and trails of ivy from the woods, and Ebba had helped them loop it along the roof beams in the Big Hall, warmly curtained for the occasion.

The farm people came up and they all waited in the yard for Renfrith until dusk was gathering and they were just about to close the gate. Then they heard the horn in the woods.

Renfrith and Beren rode in. Renfrith raised his hand. 'Good health to you and a merry Midwinter.' Stiffly, they dismounted.

'Now,' said Lady Aldswith, 'we are all ready to invoke the gods. Let us implore the Sun to return from the warm south. Let us frighten off the wolves of winter with our imprecations.'

'No,' said Renfrith. 'I cannot do it.'

'Oh, yes, you can, my son. You are head of the house. We have no priest of the gods here to make a blood sacrifice, but invocations and offerings we can make.'

'I cannot,' said Renfrith. 'I am Christ's man.'

Lady Aldswith looked alarmed. They were all dismayed. 'But we must call the Sun back.'

Renfrith turned away his head. His fists were clenched but he looked desperately weary.

Lady Aldswith held up the drinking horn and made a long invocation to the gods. There were offerings of several kinds of food and the ceremony ended with a great banging of spoons on saucepans to scare away the wolves of winter.

'Do the Scots not feast at Midwinter?' asked Lady Aldswith angrily, as they went into the Hall.

'They celebrate at this season the birth of the Lord Christ,' replied Renfrith, 'because he came as a light to our darkness.'

'Do they have such short nights or mild winters that they don't wish for the sun?'

'We have the promise of God that summer and winter, seedtime and harvest, day and night, shall not cease. And so think all Christ's men.' Renfrith steered his mother to her seat and the feast began rather grimly.

Ebba sat, pale and drooping as ever, with her large helping of pork in front of her.

'She is missing my father after all,' thought Hrethla. Orca removed Ebba's portion and put something else in front of her.

Eating improved their feelings and it was something to be able to hear some news. The Britons and the Mercians were still among the Deirans, not advancing. The king had called all his brothers together for Midwinter at Gefrin, but their followers had leave to disperse to their homes.

'Perhaps my uncle is missing his lord and all his companions,' thought Hrethla.

After the food, Renfrith brought out presents for them all. Hrethla had a little knife in a red leather sheath which fastened on her belt. She was thrilled. She had always had to borrow knives.

'You're old enough for it, Snippet,' he said. 'Don't cut your finger off and let me down, will you?'

They had some music. Beren took down the little harp that hung on the wall, but it would not work; the strings were gone. So they sang old songs, and there was more mead and more ale. Ebba looked sadder, and Lady Aldswith said ferocious things about the Mercians, the Britons and the Deirans, and the men got stupider. At last Ebba and the farm wife rose and told the children to come to bed. The children hastily seized the last of the cakes, and followed to the weaving hall, where they were to spend the night. There were beds enough and to spare, and they all turned in.

Deep in the night, Hrethla woke. Something was wrong. She crawled out and looked in her mother's bed. It was empty. She went to Orca's bed and Gil was there.

She pulled on her overdress, which was all she had taken off, and crept to the door. The yard glittered in heavy frost, and the high gate, that Sibald had barred when he let Fen out to guard the homestead, swung ajar.

Hrethla took Orca's thick woollen cape from its nail, pulled on her boots and went to the Big Hall. Overhead the silver lad that drove the moon held his chariot. He cared no more for those creatures that chewed it away from him, month after month, than her Uncle Renfrith had minded the menace of winter. The moon always came back.

Orca was in the Big Hall. She lay asleep on the edge of the bench just inside the door. Her arm was over Lady Aldswith, who was breathing as loud as a horse.

It would not do to risk waking the old lady. She usually became difficult at a feast. Hrethla only wished she had thought to guard Ebba. She wondered if other families were plagued with such problems.

She made her way past the uncleared tables and the men in their sleeping places. The dog Ban, lying by Beren, opened one eye and growled softly. This reminded her to pick up a bone. There was one other person awake, however, and watching her.

'Uncle Renfrith,' whispered Hrethla. 'My mother's gone out – Ebba. She's looking for my father's ghost. Come and help me find her.'

4 Down to the Meres

Renfrith had not been to sleep. He came carefully round the tables to Hrethla. He took her hand and they went out into the moonlight.

There was a bucket on the bench outside the Hall door. Renfrith splashed his face with icy water and sat down.

'That's better,' he said. 'Now say that again.'

Hrethla said it.

'Where?'

'She goes to the Meres,' Hrethla explained.

She could feel Renfrith's shock, but he stood up and crossed the farmyard. At the stable he stopped and collected a heavy cloak.

They went out through the half open gate, and Fen came rushing at them out of the dark.

'Good dog, good Fen,' she told him, and gave him the bone. Puzzled, he smelt it, and them, and they went on.

Most people were terrified of ghosts, but Hrethla was not afraid of her father's. As for Renfrith, she had wondered, when he objected to going after Wulfwine Wulfing, if he were really brave, but now she saw he was brave enough when the need was.

'Does your mother often do this sort of thing?' Renfrith asked.

'Only when she's upset. You upset her. She was happy. Why did you have to come home miserable?'

No answer. Then he said; 'The king has gone back to his old gods.'

'Well, he's come back to his old country.'

'It's not like that. With the gods, you do offerings and

sacrifices and so forth, and hope they'll be favourable. But with this, if you go back on the Lord Christ, it's no different from breaking faith with your own lord that leads you in battle and gives you treasure.'

Hrethla had never heard of such a god, so peculiarly like a man. She saved her breath for walking.

It was six miles through the bitter frost, and rough going. Renfrith strode along and Hrethla hurried to keep up. Her feet were like two stones that came down from her knees, where the feeling ended, and she could not tell whether her breath hurt because of the bitter air or from anxiety. Ebba had had a good start. She had nearly reached the Meres when they saw her ahead of them, a dark figure moving into the dark of the alder trees.

'What now?' whispered Renfrith, shocked again.

'Don't frighten her. I'll go and see if I can turn her round. Then you come.'

They went down the slope. Ebba turned aside at the edge of the reeds as if searching.

'Ingui. Oh, Ingui.'

Hrethla took her elbow.

'Come along, mama. He isn't here, you know. He died in his bed.'

Ebba still moaned, but she came. They steered her back to the path and set off.

Less worried, Hrethla looked up. The moon was over to the west. The stars snapped, hard as jewels, above. She glanced left and gasped.

An arch flickered out from the black sky. Green light danced upon its edge. Inside, white sheets of light grew and spread, faded and glowed again. The Frost People were at their feasting and had forgotten to shut the door.

The Frost People, as well she knew, were enemies. They sought the death of living things, and warred with the gods that kept mankind. But the beauty of their lighted halls as they kept their Midwinter feast, seen after that eerie search, remained with her all her life long.

The great arch dimmed and died away. Down off the moor they came to the gate of Hundfelth, Orca was looking out for them in the cold dark; she had Fen chained. Ebba stumbled through the gate into Orca's arms.

'My poor lamb. Come to bed,' said Orca, and to Renfrith, 'Take the child in the kitchen, you'll find what you need.'

The kitchen fire was banked up, and there was milk ready to heat. They were both drinking it when Orca came in.

'A pretty kettle of fish,' said she.

'Is it sleep-walking?' asked Renfrith.

'No, she can take these turns in broad daylight, but she's not in her right mind when she does.'

'Why is it?'

'Oh, you,' exclaimed Orca, suddenly exasperated. 'You, and that Elfric Wulfing and Redpath of course, always out and away, and Ingui seeing to the whole of the homestead, what do you expect?'

Renfrith waited.

'And then your brother comes home on a stretcher and we're told it's Wulfwine Wulfing's doing. And there's a fine to-do, my lady not wanting to take the compensation money, crying out for a killing instead. And you and Elfric off to the land of the Scots, so there's no help there.'

'Yes.'

'That poor Ebba. No wonder she wanted Ingui, and Ingui wanted her, both as lonely as you like. And did my lady fancy that, her daughter marrying a serving man? Though how Ingui came to be a serving man, I never shall know.'

'No.'

'We had the wedding anyway. The Wulfings all came too, as was proper. And my lady, you might know, must pick such a quarrel with the Wulfings that they've not been here from that day to this.'

'Ah.'

'And so it went on. Ingui had the worst of her temper then. She seemed bent on keeping those two apart. Then, it was a very cold winter, the time the child was born, and we had no end of trouble with the sheep. The wolves came in. . .'

'Mm.'

'. . . we'd have had none of the beasts left, if it hadn't been for Ingui. But the upshot was, he was down at the Meres with Wig one night, getting sheep out of the snow, and he went through the ice. Came back in the morning, and would she let him lie in the warm? He had to lie out in the hut where he'd been all winter – she'd had Ebba in the weaving hall with the babe.'

Orca seemed to have finished.

'What happened?'

'Happened? He died in his bed. Your sister never got over it. She didn't see him while he was ill either. A bad business.'

Renfrith seemed to feel it so too.

'What's meant to, happens,' said Orca. 'Twelve years you've been away, and here you come home to all this trouble, lad. It's good of you to go out after her and take care of the child. Go in the Hall and get some sleep. The others won't wake yet awhile.'

Orca had been plying him with food while she held forth. He stood up and yawned.

'Go on,' she bade him.

'Thanks, Orca,' said Renfrith. 'Good health, sister's daughter.' He kissed Hrethla's hair before going off to the Hall.

Orca took Hrethla on her lap and warmed her feet in her hands.

'How did you know, Orca?'

'I saw.' Orca put a stone in the embers. When it was hot, she wrapped it in a piece of skin, and put Hrethla in the bed in her own room with it. Hrethla slept warmly almost until dinner time.

Everything was back to normal, if you could call the Midwinter Feast normal. There were large dinners every day and the least possible work done. Everyone could sleep as long as they wanted but Hrethla did not want to. As far as she could go on foot, she went hunting with Uncle Renfrith, and he let her. She thought she could teach Snibba hunting. Ban was very nice to him.

After about a week of this, Renfrith said one evening;

'Time passes, like the shuttle on the loom. Tomorrow we must ride away to meet my Lord Oswald.'

No one was surprised but they grunted sympathetically. Lady Aldswith made a speech.

'Now are the dogs of war let loose,' she said. 'Now will Ethelfrith be avenged, and his son will overthrow his enemies and wield the power of Ida's line. Swift and violent, follow your lord into battle and win glory for your king.'

Hrethla knew about the dogs of war. They were very fierce animals, and once loose there was no telling whether they could be brought back under control. They were worse than Fen. The god of war, Tiu himself, when chaining one of them, had had his right hand bitten off and now had to fight with his left.

5 Spring of Hope

Renfrith and Beren rode away the next day. Ban stayed behind.

'He can't come to war with me,' Beren explained to Hrethla. 'Your grandmother says he may stop here. But if you look after him and be his lady, he won't miss me so much.'

'Would you like that?' Hrethla asked Ban, holding him under the chin, and he looked at her with sad eyes. But he stayed with her and Snibba when she waved goodbye from the top of the ridge, and they walked down to the farmstead together.

'They think I am their lady,' thought Hrethla. 'They will look after me and I must look after them, just like Oswald Ethelfrith's son is lord to his fighting men.'

They went everywhere with her, out on the moor, down to the woods for firewood, and round the fields, where she tried to carry on some of the good work begun by her uncle by mending the gaps in the fences. There was plenty to eat, thanks to his hunting expeditions, on some of which, she suspected, Elfric Wulfing had joined.

It was very cold, and she did not want to leave off her new dress.

'Is that child to rag those fine clothes to pieces round the farmyard?' asked Orca.

Ebba cut the blue cloth from the loom and Orca ran up a small overdress. Ebba found an old red underdress, and Orca cut it down. Hrethla put on the red and the blue, belted her red-sheathed knife on top and sat down in the straw by the fire to tend the mucky lamb Wig had brought in.

'That looks better.' Lady Aldswith approved of something for once. 'Put the child in a bit of colour, not that old thing of yours, Ebba. You always looked wishy-washy in it yourself.'

'My other dress is very nice for feast days,' said Hrethla.

'Think you're Somebody, don't you,' replied her grandmother.

Sibald came up to the house.

'I'm here to say goodbye,' he said. 'They're calling the army out. It'll be quick march tomorrow.'

Lady Aldswith gave him some charms for good luck, and told him to be sure to look out for Lord Renfrith amongst Prince Oswald's fighting men. Sibald said he didn't know that he'd see him: he was going with the men from Hagulstad (now called Hexham).

'We shall soon have those Deirans on the run,' said Lady Aldswith when he had departed.

'I thought it was the Britons we were fighting,' Hrethla remarked.

'Ah yes. Codwallop or some such name. Never mind, with Ethelfrith's son in power we shall have the good times back. I'll take you to the Midsummer Fair at Hagulstad, little Hrethla. It's time you saw a bit of life.'

'What's that like?'

'You've no idea, child. There are so many people! They all come in for the sacrifices. The priests slaughter by the sacred trees on one side of the town, pigs and oxen, and at the proper times, a horse. And in the evening everyone comes back to the fires, and feasts, and there is dancing and singing, and jumping over the fires. Then of course, there's the market!'

'What's that for?'

'Trading and dealing. Bring and barter. Everything you want but can't make for yourself – a fine needle for a fat hen, a sheep against a cooking pot. Rolls of cloth, red, blue, yellow, brown, as you need it . . .'

'But who wants cloth?'

'Some folk do. We've no lack, with the sheep. So just you get on with that wool.' Hrethla pulled some more out of the distaff and kept her fingers busy.

'. . . And livestock; hens, ducks, geese, sheep, goats, cattle, slaves, serving men . . .'

'What's the difference between a slave and a serving man?'

'Ah. A slave's got to go where he's taken. He's lost his freedom, falling into debt, or enemy hands. His master can work him, or trade him in. But a serving man can offer his services for a time, and go when he wishes.'

'It must be sad to be a slave.'

'When you're my age you'll have trouble enough without looking at other people's. See what ill luck has been mine all my life.'

'Well, you've got this homestead, and all of us.'

'That's how little you know of how things should be. When your grandfather Wictred brought me here – ah, the first year or two were hard. We lived in huts put up out of branches while the stockade was built, and the space inside seemed so large I laughed at the idea of filling it. But we took a good crop from the fresh-ploughed land. And when the settlement was established, I had all a woman could wish for, bonny cows for milking, a beautiful dairy, five looms in the weaving hall, and women to work them in all the slack times. Every day we had the tables up in the Big Hall and filled it with folk at their evening meal, and the men's beds round the walls were all used at night. And I had my children, my four lovely lads.'

'And Ebba my mother.'

'Yes, her too. And everything went well in those days. Ethelfrith Ethelric's son ruled, of the race of great King Ida, that built Bebbanburgh for his stronghold and named it after his queen. He was the first of our kings after we came across the sea in ships, with all our cattle and tools for forest and farm. There was nobody here before us.'

'What about the Romans?'

'Oh, the Romans had left long before us. Our people came sailing, emptying all the Angle-land from which we came, and took up land wherever we chose. And Ida reigned, and then Ethelric, and then Ethelfrith of widest renown. He ruled not our people only, but the Deirans, from whose royal house his wife came. And further, he was acknowledged overlord by the kingdoms far to south and west, even the border country, Mercia.

'But Edwin Alla's son, his wife's brother, whom he had exiled, came with the King of the East Englemen and his army. Ethelfrith marched to meet him, and all his loyal fighting men, Wictred and almost all the menfolk we had here, and our two eldest sons, who were just old enough to go to war. And there, far away in the south, by the Idle River, Edwin fell on them and slaughtered them. Nearly every one of our men was killed in unfaltering loyalty to their lord. As for Wictred, Matta brought him back, one of the men we had, and how he got him all that way, wounded as he was, I do not know. But he could just as well have saved his trouble, for Wictred died at the time when ploughing begins. He could just as well have fallen on the battlefield, and then Woden, wisest of the gods, might have picked him up and carried him to the halls of feasting.

'So there was I, with my two young sons, Redpath and Renfrith, and no friend to help them to manly arts and the honour of fighting men. And they spent all their time in sword-play and hunting. But then that dastardly Wulfwine took the life of one of my sons, and the other fled to the land of the Scots, and left me desolate.'

Hrethla was still thinking about her grandmother's story next morning, when she set out with supplies for Wig. Wig stayed out with the sheep during lambing time. He had a little shelter built by himself out of stones from the Wall, which Hrethla thought extraordinarily clever of him.

They discussed the lambs. Then Hrethla said, 'Where did the sheep come from, Wig?'

'The sheep. Always was here.'

'But when you came, with my grandfather, were they here then, when there weren't any people?'

'I never came with your grandad. Always was here. He let me be, gave me my old Gil out of the women that came and he set his young men to keep the wolves off. So I let him be.'

Hrethla thought a bit.

'Wig, my father, was he good with the sheep?'

'Ingui? Ay, he was. Hasn't been any of them like Ingui. Most of them, they'd take all they could, but no help to the flock whatever. Always toiling away at cutting down trees and growing their grain. No use to me.'

Hrethla thought again.

'Were the gods here always too, or did they come with the – the settlers?'

Wig thought this time.

'There now. I don't know as they did come. Could be, they stayed behind in that old Angle-land of theirs. That Woden, now, he could've. Always wandering round and poking his nose in, whether he was wanted or not, by what they say. But if he came, the likelihood is, he's gone back since. And maybe the men won't stay that long either. The way things are going, they'll knock each other to bits some day soon.'

Wig had never talked like this before; it made Hrethla feel uneasy.

6 Summer of Trouble

They heard that at Hagulstad, before the army marched away, there had been great sacrifices made to the gods. Since King Edwin had taken up 'the new religion' this had not been done. Everyone hoped that the results would be favourable.

Hrethla made herself a bow and arrows of sorts, and went out to practise shooting. Sometimes she thought she would need to fight, sometimes she had hunting in mind. Ban looked on hopefully.

The cow had twins. Orca thought that only the boy should be allowed to grow up, as a plough ox. Hrethla pleaded to keep both.

'You must look after them then,' said Orca, and Hrethla did, taking them to choice bits of pasture and feeding them with suitable grass and leaves, so that they should grow up quickly and leave more milk for the house.

Midsummer came, but Lady Aldswith did not take Hrethla to Hagulstad Fair. There were strangers down at the cottage, and she sent Ebba to find out what they wanted. Ebba took Hrethla and the dogs for company.

'They came up this morning from the river,' said the farm wife. 'The man says his name's Thurstan and his wife's Mildred. The woman doesn't say a thing. She's too done up.'

Ebba looked at the strangers, exhausted and bedraggled on the bench.

'Where do you come from?' she asked. 'And what do you want?'

'Lady,' said Thurstan, 'I haven't seen a quieter place

since King Edwin died, to our sore loss. If I could leave the wife and get back to the fighting – I'd fight, even under Ethelfrith's sons.'

'You're from Deira,' said Ebba. 'What happened?'

'There's nothing left,' he replied. 'The Britons have overrun the whole countryside; burnt everything, killed all the animals. King Edwin's nephew, the one that rallied the people last autumn, got himself shut up in a walled town with Cadwallon and his Britons outside; tried to break a way out and got cut down with all his fighting men. Some of us doubled back to the woods. We'd the women and children there. It's a wonder we got them away. The Britons never did like woods but they seem to be learning fast.'

'Where are the children?'

'Dead,' said the man, and his wife shivered.

'Hum,' said Ebba. 'You can come up to the house. But don't talk about Edwin Alla's son to my mother.'

Thurstan left them after a few days but Mildred stayed, a silent, lifeless creature, but constantly working.

These were not the only strangers.

'It's another hot day,' said Orca to Ebba, some weeks later. 'Shall we wash?'

They collected every garment and every bed-covering they could lay hands on, and took them down to the river. Hrethla followed in her old rag of a frock.

They pounded away, cleaning the clothes on the stones, and Hrethla ran about, spreading things out to dry on the grass in the clearing, when suddenly a ragged man with a broken spear came out of the bushes, and stood and laughed, long and wildly.

'You'd never think there was a war on here!' he said.

They calmed him down and took him up to the house to

be fed. His news was like Thurstan's, but the Britons had come nearer. The young king could never meet them in battle: they behaved as if the countryside was theirs to plunder and destroy.

Lady Aldswith's eyes flashed.

'What's the matter with the men today?' she demanded. 'What can we give the gods? Thunor shall have the bull calf if he gives us victory.'

There was a thunderstorm that same night. Hrethla lay in bed and heard Thunor cracking the sky open with his great hammer, moving from north to south; he should be going to the aid of the Bernicians. She felt sad about the bull calf.

Wig had sheared the sheep, filling a hut with fleeces to be spun into yarn, enough to dampen anyone's spirits, Hrethla thought, and had taken the sheep up to summer pasture. Now, a few days after the man had left them, Wig came back unexpectedly.

'Anyone coming to the hills with me till this has blown over?'

'Never,' declared Lady Aldswith, 'will I abandon this homestead, though they burn it over my head!' She glared round the half-circle of the other women as if daring them to run away.

'Have it your own way,' grunted Wig, and cleared out.

'And what has he heard?' wondered Orca.

After this they began to lose things. At the cottage eggs disappeared. A pig went missing. They harvested by dribs and drabs, bringing in what they had cut to dry out in the yard. Left to lie in the field, it disappeared.

The farming men caught some vagabonds. They said they had lost their way, trying to join up with the army. That time they told them to ask, not steal, and gave them food. But the next set that came were just marauders, out to get what they could; they were thrashed and sent packing.

The weather broke and autumn set in early, with days of drizzle and heavy mist. A day came when the mist closed in not long after mid-day. Hrethla brought the cow in, and Duffa came up the field path driving the six young sows which they now shut up every night.

They loosed Fen early, barred the gate, and were ready to eat dinner in the weaving hall, when suddenly they heard a scream, piercing, long-drawn.

Orca closed the door fast. Gil and Ebba doused the fire. They sat almost in darkness, listening to a confused and horrible noise, away, somewhere, in the fog.

Stealthily, as if they might be seen or heard, they pushed the door open and went out to look. Beyond the gate the fog was smudged with orange. This grew brighter, and between the noises they heard the crackling of fire.

Late into the night they watched and listened to this dreadful bonfire, but the noise never came nearer to them. In the grey morning they crept out to see what had happened.

The cottage and its outbuildings were a blackened heap, still smoking. The cultivated ground all round was trampled flat. A round black patch in front had been a cooking fire, but not all the beasts had been eaten in one night. The rest lay dead. Only the framework of the unbuilt barn stood, and from the roof tree dangled two bundles. The raiders had hanged the farming men from that beam; the wife and children perished in the fire.

There was no sign of the murderers.

They came back to the farmstead and stayed in all day. They made the animals as comfortable as they could in their stalls. They looked at one another, and Hrethla looked at each of the grown-ups in turn. But they did not say what they all thought: is it out turn next? And should we have a better chance if we went away across the moor?

The mist hung about all day, and all night nothing happened.

It was Orca who first noticed the dull roaring sound early next morning.

'What's that now?' They all listened; a great many people were making a great deal of noise a long way off. Lady Aldswith had the answer.

'There's a battle.'

Once again they did not unbar the gate but stayed in the yard listening to the distant clamour which seemed to be down the river, to the south where the Wall crossed it. All morning it went on.

'If only we could see something.'

'I'm going to have a look,' said Hrethla.

She hauled the ladder up against the fence, climbed to the top and scrambled into the ash tree. Standing among the boughs she could certainly see some way over the moor above the house. After a long while she called down;

'There's a man coming. It's Uncle Renfrith.'

7 Battle in Autumn

'Uncle Renfrith! Uncle Renfrith!' called Hrethla.

He stopped and looked up in the tree.

'You're safe?' he exclaimed. 'Thank God!'

'What's happened?'

'Tell them to undo the gate. We're winning. The Britons are on the run. But we want to bring the wounded here.'

Later that afternoon, Orca remarked, 'Never let it be said that nobody ever comes to this place.'

Renfrith had not been back, but Sibald had come several times as part of a stretcher party. Elfric Wulfing was one he brought in, looking as beautiful as ever, with gold hair, white face and closed eyes. Hrethla thought he must be dead, but he had only lost a lot of blood.

Beren came in on his feet, but so knocked about and dirty that only Ban recognized him. His arm was quite out at the shoulder, but Orca and a man who came with him had him down on the straw and pushed his shoulder back together again. Ban was very suspicious of the whole thing, and they left him, licking Beren's face, while Beren got over it.

They put the men in the Big Hall, lying in rows at right angles to the wall, and as Orca said, it was a comfort to see all that straw being put to good use. There were twenty to thirty men in the Hall by nightfall when Prince Oswald rode in to see how things stood.

The Prince seemed to have lost his iron battle cap and his fair hair was all blown about. He looked very tired, but happy, and smiled at them with kind eyes as he went in to see the men. Hrethla decided he was much, much nicer-looking than Elfric Wulfing.

The men cheered him as he rode away to see to the main camp. He was clearly the hero of the battle. Hrethla wondered how her uncle's lord came to be leading the army, and what had happened to his older brother who was king, but it was some days before she heard the full story.

'Frig help us,' muttered Lady Aldswith, as she looked at the Hall full of wounded men. Hrethla supposed that Frig, a lady among the gods, and Woden's wife, was the right one to invoke, though she had never, herself, liked what she heard about her. She seemed only too keen to keep little girls at their spinning. But Aldswith and Ebba were not really upset by the turn of events. Ladies were expected to know how to deal with injuries.

Ebba was always pleased when people needed looking after, and Orca had a wonderful time using all her herbs and potions. Hrethla fetched and carried and did as she was told, and learnt quite a lot in the process.

Some of the men were up and away quite soon. Elfric Wulfing was one. He thanked Lady Aldswith gracefully for her hospitality, and went away before she had quite realised who he was, much to the relief of Orca, who had kept her well away from him.

Beren, however, was in pain. Besides his dislocated shoulder he had his collar bone and several ribs broken. They bandaged his arm to his chest and propped him up against a bale of straw. He said he felt better.

'Tell me about the battle,' said Hrethla. 'But not if it hurts.'

'It'll take my mind off my shoulder,' said Beren.

'Have you been fighting the Britons all through the summer?' asked Hrethla, while Ban rested his nose on Beren's knee, happy at having his two favourite people together.

'We've hardly had any fighting,' explained Beren. 'The king was so angry with Lord Oswald, because he would not forswear the Lord Christ and go back to the old gods, that he put him to garrison the castle of Bebbanburgh, just with his own followers. And there we were stuck, while the King chased up and down the country, trying to get to grips with the enemy.'

Beren stopped for some breathing, and Hrethla went on spinning.

'It's been a funny war,' said Beren. 'Normally the Britons keep to high ground and open country. This time they've fought in lowland and forests and towns. It's been Englemen against Englemen, too, because the Mercians have been fighting with the Britons, though their leader does seem to have gone home. He's a deep one, that Penda. And then the Britons usually quarrel with each other, and scatter their forces when they go on their long-distance raids. But not this time.'

'Did they do long-distance raids this time?'

'They did. They came up the coast one night and we never knew it until they were all past the fortress. We caught them coming back two nights later. That was one time they didn't return to Cadwallon. But in the meantime they had sacked Gefrin and burnt the palace out.

'It was only a few days after that when we had some real news. The king had gone to try to make terms with Cadwallon, he and twelve companions. They were all murdered. What was left of the troops was scattered.

'I thought, "This is the end. We shall have to go back to the Scots." But Prince Oswald questioned the messenger, and then he said, "So it falls to me to avenge my brother. How do we surprise Cadwallon? He'll expect us down the coast road."

'He ordered everything to be packed up, and he sent me off with the messenger along the coast, to pick up all the fighting men and soldiers we could find, and bring them over the moors to meet him. So we did.'

'Where did Prince Oswald go?'

'He marched westwards into the hills to Gefrin in its ruins. People came out of hiding and joined him. Then he turned south along the Dera Street, as far as the old Roman camp at Habitancum, where we were to meet. We camped nearby.'

No Englemen would have camped on the old Roman site itself, because of the ghosts, as Hrethla knew. 'Did you have many fighting men?' she asked.

'Not as many as we had hoped for. We made a very small army. But it was something to see old faces and to hear some news. We met a man called Thurstan; he told us Hundfelth was still standing in the summer, for he'd left his wife there. And next day, when we were on the march again, your Sibald found out Renfrith.

'We came over the moors through the mist, and Cadwallon was pulling all his forces together in the river valley. Queer, wasn't it? We slept, some of us did anyway, on the hill that night, no fires, no cooked meat, no talk or singing. We did some more scouting, and we caught a few scouts, so we knew tomorrow was the day.

'Your Sibald did a spot of scouting on his own, to see how his family were getting on. He found the place burnt out, as you know. He and the lads with him managed to bury his brothers; they brought back a beam of wood, charred, for evidence of what had happened.

'Before it was properly light, we started lining up, ready for battle. One of the old warriors, Ethelfrith's man, was urging the prince to make a fighting speech before the battle. And that, Lord Oswald had never done. He just said, "Yes, we have to know what we're fighting for. Let's have a standard."

'He saw Sibald with his beam and fetched him forward, and we soon had another piece of wood to make a cross. We stuck it in the ground, and Prince Oswald held it steady while we stamped the earth down.

'He told the troops, "Today we have to fight a cruel enemy who has taken our country, our goods, and the lives of our people. And this is the standard we shall fight under, the Cross of Christ. We make no other sacrifice; His sacrifice alone avails for men." And in front of all the men, he knelt and prayed.'

Hrethla did not know why the Cross should stand for Christ, but, like Oswald's army, she took the point. Prince Oswald, like Uncle Renfrith, had not broken faith with the Lord Christ.

'Then he stood up and drew his sword and shouted "For Christ and Bernicia," and away we went down the hill to join battle.

'We caught them by surprise, all right. We pressed them down towards the river, and fought in the ford; they gave way and rallied on the other side, against the Wall. That was where the hard fighting began, and you heard the noise here. The sun came out, and we began to drive them along the Wall. Some of them ran, but some of them turned and fought fiercely enough, like the one that knocked me about. Cadwallon was killed, down by the Denise's burn, and then, of course, they did run. But before that, Lord Oswald came across Renfrith and told him to find somewhere that would take the wounded, knowing, of course, that it was his home ground.'

'What will happen now?' asked Hrethla, when she had given Beren time to rest.

'Lord Oswald will give a Feast,' said Beren. 'And I shan't be there. And then the old men will get together and choose him to be king in his brother's stead.'

'Will they?'

'The men wouldn't stand for it if they didn't. But they will anyway.'

8 Friends and Neighbours

Renfrith came home after the victory feast, and brought Beren's share of the gifts which Oswald had given, like a good lord, to his loyal followers. The army dispersed, and Oswald the King went to Bebbanburgh with some of the fighting men and the older men of high position in the land of the Bernicians. The men who had recovered left Hundfelth, except one or two who had no homes now to go to. They stayed on, working on the farm, and sleeping in the Big Hall, like Sibald, Beren and Renfrith. Thurstan, too stayed with them.

It was time to plough, and they had no oxen. Renfrith put his horse and Beren's to draw the plough, and drove it himself. Hrethla pitied the horses, put to hard service in the mud, and Thurstan said it was as well the soil was light and poor here, not like it was further south.

'Whatever happens, you must plough,' said Renfrith. 'If I'd no horses, I'd yoke up you and Duffa. Men have had to draw the plough before now.' So Thurstan went back to digging Orca's garden, and Hrethla to minding the cow and practising shooting with the bow her uncle had found for her.

Renfrith never stopped doing things. After a day's work he went over to the Wulfings or out hunting. Wig had come back shortly after the battle, but Renfrith would not let him start the autumn slaughtering. He brought in meat from the hills, and took the surplus sheep to Hagulstad market, with a good many pigs and both the calves. He said there would be plenty of people wanting stock to put on their grazing ground, because grazing was all they had left.

Hrethla was glad to think that the calves would live to grow up. Nor did she mind when Renfrith asked Ebba why she was storing up so much wool for the maggots, and took that off to market too.

He brought back new tools and cooking pots, replacing things that had broken or worn out, or had been lost with the cottage. Lady Aldswith wanted him to bring back a priest, so as to get some luck about the house. Renfrith laughed.

'I can't be ahead of the king. He has sent to the Scots' land for a priest. And here too, when we have one, it shall be one that's Christ's man.'

'Well,' pursued Lady Aldswith, 'now the fighting's over, you can finish off Wulfwine Wulfing.'

'If that business is not settled, it certainly must be,' replied Renfrith, and he rode off to the Wulfings.

Beren improved slowly. He was not fit for farm work but he could use his fingers. He mended harness, and made the little Hall harp work, and he made Hrethla good arrows for her bow. He also made her a necklace of wooden beads which she had for a present at Midwinter.

Renfrith announced that they would not invoke the gods this year, but he and Beren would take Christian prayers in the Hall. Lady Aldswith strictly forbade any of the women to be there. Thurstan, Sibald and the other men promptly decided to join Renfrith in the Hall.

When the Feast came round, Lady Aldswith gathered the women in the yard and intoned the proper words with great fervour. But Hrethla kept remembering that last year, even at his most hopeless, Uncle Renfrith had been sure that the Living God would see to it that the sun came back every year. To her the incantations all sounded like a worn-out spell. It was clear also that the gods had been no earthly use to the Bernicians and the Deirans in the war.

The feast itself was very cheerful, with plenty to eat and drink, plenty of firewood, plenty of fun and music, with each man taking a turn at the harp and singing old songs. Only there was no family to come up from the cottage, and Sibald had time to grieve.

Two mornings later, when Hrethla came out of the weaving hall, she found her uncle and Beren saddling their horses, and Renfrith said: 'Come to the Wulfings with us, Snippet.'

'Oh, please.'

She had her pretty patterned dress on, and she ran in to fetch her new beads and cloak. Orca was raking up the fire. Hrethla glanced at her grandmother, in bed and still asleep.

'Do you think I ought to go to the Wulfings with Uncle Renfrith, Orca?'

Orca stood up and tidied Hrethla's hair.

'It's plain your uncle doesn't mean us to go on living all shut up as we have been. And this being a Saturday, which is a day dedicated to a god of feasting and jollification, what better day to go?'

'You've grown, Snippet,' said Renfrith. 'You can't perch on my saddlebow this year. Come up behind.'

So Hrethla sat behind him and had a sideways view of the fields and the woods. She thought perhaps this exciting outing was instead of a present; her uncle had not given her anything this year.

'Will the Wulfings mind me coming too?'

'I've told them I'm bringing you. Freagifu will like to see you.'

'Who is Freagifu?'

'Elfric's little sister.'

Riding steadily for Beren's sake, they came through the

woods to the ploughed land. Here Renfrith blew his horn, and they went on across the big brown field, neatly striped, towards the spacious well-fenced homestead and group of cottages, with green meadowland sloping to the river, and a burn coming down off the moor. The Wulfings settlement was all that Hundfelth should have been.

Elfric Wulfing came out.

'Good health, Giltbeard.'

'Good health, Sharpshooter. Glad to see you, Bright-fingers. You'll soon be as good as new. Is this the little sister's daughter?'

'Yes, shall we take her in to Freagifu?'

Elfric's little sister looked grown up to Hrethla. She was like him, with long crinkly golden plaits. Hrethla was glad her own hair was in pigtails; it made all the combing worthwhile. Freagifu kissed Hrethla and said she must sit beside her at the table, because she was a visitor. They were just going in to the mid-day meal.

Renfrith sat on the other side of Hrethla, and she ate as nicely as she knew how and gazed at the large Hall full of people, children standing clustered at the end of the tables, farming folk munching comfortably at the feast-time food, and the family of the farmstead.

She looked carefully at Wulfwine, who had killed her uncle. He seemed to be the mildest looking of the three Wulfing brothers, sitting at the top of the table with huge moustaches and straggling grey plaits getting in their food and drinking horns. The young men, Elfric's brothers and cousins, were copying the new fashions from the Scots' land, and wore their hair short, combed out on their shoulders. The older women wore long plaits too, which showed under their headscarves, but Freagifu had only a ribbon in her hair, matching her eyes and her blue-green dress. 'How many people there are in the world,' thought Hrethla, 'all living different lives that weave in and out of each other without knowing it. And does it all join up somewhere into a proper pattern?'

Old and young, the Wulfing men talked about horses, and when the meal was over, they went out to look at horses, taking Renfrith with them.

Freagifu went over to the little girls and introduced Hrethla. They stayed, talking, in the Big Hall, until Renfrith called: 'Snippet!'

Hrethla ran out and found him standing by a little dark pony, saddled.

'Want a ride?'

'Oh, please.' Hrethla had her foot in the stirrup.

'Oh, Renfrith,' protested Freagifu. 'Mind her skirt.'

Hrethla hitched up her skirt and sprang astride the pony. Renfrith laughed. 'Can you ride him home? He's yours.'

'Not really?'

'Yes, from me, only he must help on the farm when he's needed.'

So Hrethla rode her own pony home through the woods and up the field path and in at the gate as the frost came down with nightfall.

'And where have you been, you impudent little vagabond?'

Hrethla sat still and looked at Lady Aldswith, and her skin got ready for a beating.

'Out.'

'And where did you get that animal, may I ask?' Renfrith strode across the yard.

'I gave it to her. I bought it.'

'From the Wulfings! You insult me. You are afraid of Wulfwine. Or else you'll only fight behind that fine lord of yours. Not for your family. You good-for-nothing coward.'

The word she used was the worst of insults.

'Mother,' said Renfrith, cold and hard. 'I've told you before. I'm telling you now in front of everybody. The matter is closed. It was settled in the court at Hagulstad. Ingui stood witness for you. He's dead, and other witnesses are dead or lost, but I believe Wulfwine, for no-one regrets Redpath's death more. It is you, distraught with sorrow, that has forgotten. I did wrong to run off to the Scots' land and leave you, but I tell you, if you raise this matter once more, I'm away again; I'll serve Oswald as his fighting man, and home I will not come; you can manage the place by yourself. And in the meantime, I shall stay friends with the Wulfings.'

Lady Aldswith stood and screamed, and screamed.

'Ungrateful son!'

She stamped off to the weaving hall, and slammed the door, while all the household stood and watched the proceedings.

Renfrith went slowly into the Big Hall, and sat down in his place with his head in his hands.

9 New Relations

Lady Aldswith remained in the weaving hall, and in a very bad temper, for the rest of the feast. But, as Orca said, 'seeing it's young Renfrith, she'll get over it,' and one day she appeared in her place at dinner as if nothing had happened.

Before the month was out Renfrith announced at dinner one evening that he had asked Wulfgar Wulfing for Freagifu his daughter as wife and Wulfgar had agreed. Lady Aldswith looked black as thunder, but the men congratulated Renfrith, clapped him on the back, drank his health, and the women approved, so she did not stand against it.

The winter's work was going well by this time. Thurstan put up the frame of a cottage north of the main buildings, on the opposite side from the old cottages. Sibald planned a one-room dwelling and workshop close by. Coming back from taking supplies to Wig at the lambing, Hrethla met Renfrith driving four sturdy oxen home from Hagulstad.

'Now we can plough up the new ground,' he said.

'How did you get those?' asked Hrethla.

'With some of the rings that my dear lord gave me.'

'Oh, is that what the king's gifts are for?' Hrethla saw that these fine ring-givings after battles could be very useful. Later Renfrith brought home a fine cow especially as a wedding present for Freagifu. Cows were very valuable that year.

Hrethla went several times to Wulfings and came to know the little girls quite well. Orca went too, to see about some of the arrangements.

'Orca seems to know the people here,' said Hrethla to Freagifu.

'Of course,' Freagifu laughed. 'We all know Orca. We couldn't fall out with her just because your grandmother took a huff. She's useful when people are sick. And how do you think you get your honey and your calves?'

There were no bees and no bull at Hundfelth, but Hrethla had never thought about that. How curiously people's lives were joined together, she reflected.

Elfric rode over one Sunday for Christian prayers in the Hall with Renfrith and Beren. He said the king had sent for a priest to teach the people about the Lord Christ. But when the man came he found the Englemen not fit to understand the Gospel, more like brute beasts. Renfrith made a face.

'You will be careful at the wedding, won't you, Sharp-shooter?' warned Elfric. 'I mean, my father is going to be very upset if he can't do all the usual sacrifices and things.'

'Yes, it's his daughter he's giving me. If I could wait to get married until Lord Oswald has made Christ's men of us all, it would be different,' said Renfrith regretfully.

The snow melted, the frosts grew lighter, and the wind romped across the moors. Hrethla's namesake month came and went, and the month of Easter came. It was time for the wedding.

Hrethla rode her own pony across to the Wulfings, but she was to walk back. The pony would be needed to bring a load of the bride's belongings, with the other horses that were Freagifu's wedding portion.

Hrethla waited with the Wulfing children holding spring flowers in the yard full of people. Freagifu came out of the Weaving Hall with the women of the house, and stood beside her father. The horses came galloping in at the gate, and Renfrith and his groomsmen, mostly the bride's brothers and cousins, dismounted, all in their finest clothes and polished battle gear, and came grandly across the courtyard.

Hrethla should have taken good note of the ceremonies that followed, the first wedding she had seen, and as it turned out, the last she was to see conducted in the old pagan way. But at the time, all she saw was her uncle, splendid and manly, with his quiet face, standing opposite Wulfgar, and Freagifu, beautiful as a princess in a story, with her sky-blue dress, deeply patterned at the borders, over a yellow underdress of finest wool. A high crown of golden wire and shining stones was on her head and her golden hair was brushed out, bright and crinkly, to her waist.

Hrethla very much enjoyed the feast that followed. She had a seat on a bench, with another little girl. There was plenty of food and drink and music and speeches and jokes, and afterwards people got up and began to dance.

Ebba was sitting on Hrethla's other side and began to have a strange, fixed look, which worried Hrethla. In the midst of the noise and the moving about, she stood up and began to go towards the door. Hrethla looked about for Orca, who was deep in conversation with some cottage women, so Hrethla went out with her mother.

In the open air, Ebba paused and looked about, puzzled.

'Time for bed, mama,' said Hrethla, and holding her sleeve, brought her into the weaving hall. There was a woman there who showed them where they could lie down, and Ebba slept, snoring, through the rest of the noise and the women coming in.

But early in the morning, when most people were still sleeping off the feast, she rose, and made blindly for the door, taking no notice at all of Hrethla's attempts to check her. She set out across the ploughed land, and Hrethla and Snibba beside her had to hurry to keep up.

They had reached the edge of the wood when Hrethla glanced behind and saw a man riding along the track and a great dog padding behind. It was Beren, and Hrethla was not sorry to see him.

'I see you have made an early start, Lady Ebba,' he said, dismounting. 'You will have work to do before you welcome home the bride. Will you not take a lift? The horse is very quiet.' Without any fuss, he helped Ebba on to the horse's back.

'Did you enjoy the wedding?' he asked, among the trees.

'Oh,' said Ebba in a faraway voice, 'I hope – I hope she will be happy, not like me.'

'It reminded you of your wedding,' suggested Beren. Getting no answer, he continued, 'Was that at Hundfelth?'

'At Hundfelth, yes. But different. My father was dead, and Ingui had no family.'

Beren spoke as musingly as Ebba, while Hrethla walked as quietly as she could by the horse's head, listening with all her ears. 'I had a friend called Ingui once. He died in battle. Tell me about your Ingui.'

'He was kind,' said Ebba. 'His hands were kind. He came to do the harvest and the ploughing. My mother found him at Hagulstad. After my father took my two big brothers to the war, there were not enough men on the place. And Renfrith and Redpath were only twelve and fourteen winters old.

'But after Ingui came it was better. That was the second harvest after my father died. He could do anything on the farm. And my brothers liked him. They discussed everything with him, the horses, the dogs, and the hunting. No-one knew the wild things on the moor like Ingui did. Only about the Scots' land they never talked to Ingui.

'They knew he would be there to mind the farm. They never said they meant to leave. But one day, they gave out they were going for a day or two's hunting with Elfric. They were always doing things with Elfric. But they were going away.

'They camped in the fields the first night, and they met Wulfwine. He was bringing some ponies south. The Wulfings always dealt with horses, and we at Hundfelth used to breed hunting dogs. And Redpath started to fool about with the ponies. He was like that. Headstrong. There was a scuffle, and Wulfwine's knife dropped, and it went in Redpath's throat.

'Wulfwine was dreadfully upset. He offered Renfrith the compensation there and then. But Renfrith was only sixteen. He said, "Take it to my mother. Take him to my mother."

'So they set off home. But on the way, Elfric and Renfrith came to Wulfwine and said, "We were going to the land of the Scots and we are going now, though it must be without our friend" . . . And off they went.

'So my mother would not believe that Wulfwine meant no harm. There was trouble upon trouble. But Ingui went to the Meeting with her and it was supposed to be all told and finished with.'

'Did she take the compensation?'

'I don't know. I don't remember. I was very miserable. The only reason I stayed alive then was because Ingui was kind to me.'

'He was kind to you?'

'Yes, and then presently, he wanted us to get married. My mother was cross about it, but she was always cross about things I did, anyway.

'But Ingui and I were happy. It seems funny, but I think he was lonely too, for all he had the farm and everything to see to. He wasn't just kind; he wanted me for his friend.

59

And about the baby he was very pleased.

'But that winter was bad. Everything froze. The wolves came in, and Ingui was out hunting them, night after night.

'And the baby came. "We'll call her Hrethla, for Spring," he said. "Spring will come again."

'And it snowed. Feet deep. And I lay in the weaving hall and wanted Ingui, and Ingui never came.

'He caught cold rescuing the sheep. He was ill, and he died in his bed, like my father, and I never saw him again.'

'He died for the sheep,' murmured Beren.

'He died in his bed.'

'But he was brave.'

'No, he was no good after all. He died in his bed.'

'He was very brave and very kind,' said Beren, quite loudly. 'And I am glad he had this happiness, you and the little girl.'

They came up the field path in silence. Inside the gate, Ebba slid off the horse and said; 'Thank you very much.' She put her arm round Hrethla, and looked at her with sensible eyes.

Beren hesitated. 'Lady Ebba, don't say if you'd rather not, but have you anything that belonged to your husband?'

'A few old clothes, and an old sword.'

'Would you mind, perhaps, showing me the sword?'

'I'll see.'

Beren went to put the horse away. Lady Aldswith was baking.

'Oh. You're back,' she greeted them.

Ebba looked in the best room, made ready for Renfrith and Freagifu. She went to the weaving hall, and rummaged in a box of hers.

'Go and get Beren,' she told Hrethla.

Beren sat just inside the weaving hall. Ebba put a long bundle wrapped in rags across his knees. He undid it and drew from a crude wooden case a fine sword blade. The hilt was of ancient design, a boar's head in a tangle of interlaced twigs.

'It was his emblem,' said Ebba. 'He wouldn't eat pig.'

Beren looked up. 'He could well have been my friend.'

'No,' said Ebba, sharply. 'Your friend was more fortunate. He died in battle.'

'I wonder. He was left for dead. What would a man do, if he woke to find his king dead and his comrades gone, himself in the hands of the enemy?'

'He would send to his relations, and get himself ransomed.'

'Ingui could not have done,' said Beren. 'There could be no home-going for him while Edwin reigned. He was of Ida's line. His father was first cousin to Ethelfrith. I was his foster-brother.'

'He would have gone to the Scots' land.'

'I do not know,' said Beren. 'He might be sick of battles and kingdoms. My Ingui loved every wild thing, and the changing seasons of the farm like his own life. If he escaped and found an outlying farm where he could remain unknown, I think he might indeed have been content to stay there.'

10 Hagulstad Fair

At Midsummer, Renfrith took them to the fair.

He and Freagifu rode together, laughing and teasing each other as usual. Hrethla had not known that grown-ups could play with each other like that. But Freagifu was a good worker. She took over the dairy work, and managed it well, and still had time to help Ebba at the loom. Lady Aldswith had the kitchen to herself for the baking and the cooking. She was often in a bad temper, but she took it out on Ebba as usual, so hardly anyone noticed. Ebba saw to the brewing, because of the heavy pans.

Orca was free to tend the beans and cabbages and to range the moor for herbs. And Hrethla was happy and busy all day long, minding the cows, gathering wood, and helping on the farm. She went with Freagifu to visit the Wulfings, and on Sundays they went to prayers in the Big Hall. They could not understand much, as Renfrith and Beren knew the prayers in Scots, or in the Roman tongue, in which they were known throughout the world, and were afraid of getting them wrong by putting them in Engle speech, though they added explanations. But it was a good feeling, peaceful but crisp, like a day with a clear sky and adventure ahead.

And now Hrethla rode with Renfrith and Freagifu and Sibald, down the river bank to the South River and its ford, and along the far bank to Hagulstad.

Building upon building crowded and clustered beside the wide track, big gabled halls, cottages and lean-to sheds, bothies like the separate sleeping rooms at Hundfelth, many damaged, and many mended with new wood since the

Britons came last year. Past these they rode into a place full of people, where they stopped and tied the horses to some convenient posts.

This was the market place, and here were the stalls of which Hrethla had been told, tables with a leather curtain rigged overhead and things for sale. Here were the rolls of cloth, here were shoes and slippers, and here were buckets and pots and jugs, from which Freagifu chose the things she wanted for the dairy. The men had gone to look at animals, and Freagifu traded in an old bent knife and got a needle for Hrethla's very own, safe in its little sheath, with a file to brighten it and a loop to thread on her belt.

When they had done all they wanted, they took the horses to a meadow outside the town to eat their food. Here they met a family they had seen on the way down. These people knew Sibald, and later on, when Renfrith and Freagifu sauntered back towards the town, Sibald took the oldest girl, Hrosli, and Hrethla to see the sights – the old grove where they used to sacrifice, and the Field of Meeting where complaints were heard and payment settled.

When they came back to the market place the stalls had been taken down. A man was turning cartwheels and walking on his hands to make people laugh. A crowd came jostling behind them and someone called out, 'And what sport can you make us, fellow?'

They turned, and saw a strange man who said in a strange accent, 'Sport? But I have news.'

'He was with the king's men. Here, say, is it true what's going around, that the king will be here to-night?'

The stranger looked intently at the questioner.

'The King. . . I have not Engle. . .'

He looked away, across the crowd, and suddenly cried, 'Ho there! Renfrith Sharpshooter.'

Renfrith came pushing through, handing Freagifu towards Sibald and the girls, and grasped the man's hands.

They spoke to each other in Scots, and jumped onto a table that had been a stall. The stranger began to speak, short sentences in Scots, and Renfrith gave the Engle words whenever he paused, like this:

'The king indeed is coming . . . and should be here by nightfall . . . but I am here at his request . . . I am from Hy, where your kind lived among the Scots . . . Aidan is my name. I come to tell you of the Living God . . . He it is that made the sheltering sky . . . this Middle Earth in which we dwell . . . the sea to its uttermost parts . . . and every living thing . . . there is no God but he . . .'

Hrethla listened to her uncle's voice, but she watched the stranger, Aidan of Hy (which is the Isle of Iona). He was bald and long bearded, in a long woollen coat, but his eyes held the crowd, and his radiant face was their proof that his news was real.

'All good things God has given to mankind . . . the creatures of the high hills and the wild woods, those of field and farmyard . . . all green things for food and other needs . . . the snow and storms of winter, and summer's rain and sun . . . In the beginning it was even better, . . . for when God made the world, not out of something that was here before, but by himself and for his own pleasure . . . everything was in its proper season, fair and good . . . then God made mankind, the man and the woman . . . and set them in the gladdest of gardens . . . No toil it was to till that garden . . . no animal but was as bonny and as biddable as your best of dogs . . . the fruit of all trees was good to eat . . . But one charge God laid on them, one thing they should not eat . . .

'One tree was in the middle of the Garden . . . the Tree of the Knowledge of Good and Evil . . . that fruit was forbidden them . . .

'Now the serpent was more crafty than any creature . . .

It came to the woman ... "Eat." said the serpent. "You will become like gods and know good and evil" ... The woman ate that fruit and gave it to her husband ... sure enough, they knew good and evil ... Good was all they knew before, and had not known they knew it ... evil they knew now and could not unknow it ... they nor their children, nor any generation of mankind until now ... evil of the loss of that fair Garden ... of the willing friendship of the beasts ...'

'Except only the dear dogs,' thought Hrethla.

'Evil of storms and sickness ... failure of crops and danger of poisonous plants and animals ... evil of quarrels with neighbours and cruelties in families ... evil of robbery, murder and wasteful war ...

'My friends, you have sacrificed to many gods, and little good have you had of it ... for mankind lost the knowledge of the true God when he broke his bond and ate what was forbidden ...

'But this is the good news ... In the due time, God himself came to do battle with the evil that mankind had fallen into ... God became a Man ... not in mere seeming, or as a traveller passing ... But God came as a Woman's Baby ... and lived our life on this earth beneath the sky ... and knew all the sorrows mankind is subject to ...This was in the days of the Romans, and this Man ... God, the Lord Christ, died by the Roman death ... they took him and nailed him on a wooden cross ... so he knew death as all men have known it ... it was a Warrior's death, at his foes' hands ...

'But he won the battle, he destroyed the evil, he rose to life from the dead ...'

Renfrith stopped, and Aidan stopped. Everyone turned to see what they were looking at. There in the market square stood Oswald himself, bright-faced, with his company and horses a little way behind. He saluted their cheers and came through the crowd to say laughing to Aidan. 'So my friend, you could not wait for me, but must preach, and found old Sharpshooter to do the translation.'

'Oh, my lord,' Renfrith tumbled himself off the table. 'Do you do this too?'

'Be sure I do, wherever he comes. But he won't put up with it long, he is learning the Engle too fast. Is this your wife, Renfrith? They told me you were growing an old farmer. And this young lady, I saw her at your house. Is he good to you, the old farmer? Does he beat you much?' Hrethla laughed, and skipped, holding Freagifu's hand.

They spent the evening by King Oswald's camp fire, outside the town, and heard how Aidan had come to Bernicia instead of the first teacher of whom Elfric had spoken. They spent the night at Hagulstad, Renfrith with his old comrades, Hrethla and Freagifu in a barn for all the women and children who needed a sleeping place.

When they came out next morning, itchy and far from fresh-feeling, Renfrith said, 'The king is going on a long journey, and has asked me to go, to replace a man that is sick. Do you think you can manage the packages, going home?'

ll Bebbanburgh Calling

They rode home with Freagifu in a bad mood. She declared that Renfrith must be tired of her to go off like that. Lady Aldswith informed her that she should be proud to see her lord ride after his lord, and win honour, but Freagifu retorted that even her food tasted loathsome without her loved one. Orca said she would go with her to the Wulfings to see if her sister could talk some sense into her, and when they came back, Freagifu was certainly less sulky and more disposed to take her share of the work. This was just as well, for with Renfrith away they all had more to do. Lady Aldswith enjoyed giving all the orders in his absence, but no one else found it particularly agreeable, and they realised that Renfrith had a way of tackling the most difficult jobs and coming up with the best ideas.

Lady Aldswith would not let Beren have prayers in the Hall on Sundays, so he took to going off on the moor with Ban all that day. The cottages at the back of the farmstead were finished, and the people moved out to live in them. Wig took his flock off to the hills, but not before planning a new sheepfold out by the cottages. Sibald went out in the long evening.

They made hay and began harvesting the barley. All day long they were hard at work in the fields, taking advantage of the fine weather. It seemed to stretch out for weeks.

One day, coming up from the field with an empty bucket, Hrethla found Beren on the bench by the Hall door.

'I'm a lazy old man,' he ran himself down.

'You aren't,' said Hrethla. 'I know you. It's your

shoulder playing up. What are you thinking about?'

'Bebbanburgh,' he answered promptly.

Hrethla sat down to spin. Nobody could say she was wasting time.

'Do you want to go back to Bebbanburgh?'

'I shall, one of these days.'

'Did you live there when you were a little boy?'

'No, in the hills by Gefrin.'

'Don't you want to go back to Gefrin, then? Haven't you any relations?'

'Yes, my uncle, with his farm, and six strong cousins to work it. I shall go to Bebbanburgh to serve the king.'

'Had you any brothers and sisters?'

'No, only Ingui my foster brother, and my father was steward to Ingui's father.'

'Tell me about when you and Ingui were little.'

Beren thought. 'I will tell you a story my mother used to tell Ingui and me, by the fire on winter evenings – the tale of the Worm of the Sands.

'Once upon a time, there was a castle by the sea, and in that castle lived a king, his son and his daughter and the queen their stepmother who was as wicked as she was beautiful. Indeed, she was a witch. She set the king against his son, so that he banished the young man to a distant land. She kept the princess almost a prisoner in a little hut in the courtyard. Then one day she saw that the princess had grown more beautiful than herself. She shut herself up in her room and worked some spells – and nobody saw the princess any more.

'But now a great trouble rose to vex the land. A hideous worm, a dragon, came haunting the sands beside the sea, and preyed upon the beasts of all the farms round about. It laid everything waste.

'Now the king's son heard of this in his exile, and he swore to rid his father's land of this plague. With his bold companions, he set sail in a ship, whose mast was made of the rowan tree, which is proof against witchcraft. They had no trouble finding the monster, for it came raging to the shore as they approached, and the king's son leapt into the shallows with his sword ready drawn.

'But when he reached it, the great Worm bent its head, and he heard a strange whisper. "Oh, kiss me, only kiss me."

'Then the king's son kissed the Worm, not once, not twice, but three times over; into the sand the creature sank like foam and vanished. In its place rose up a fair maiden, the king's daughter, the sister of that young hero.

'So those two went hand in hand to the castle and everyone who saw them rejoiced, and the king welcomed them. But as for the wicked witch, he banished her for ever and a day.'

'Ah,' said Hrethla in the long silence. 'Is it a true story?'

'Do you think so?' Beren's question was answer enough. 'It is an old story. I think it came across the sea with our people. But when my mother told it, I always saw Bebban-burgh and the sands of Spindlestone beyond. Though as for the young hero, and how he delivered his sister from the enchantment, that is like a foreshadowing of something that really happened. For so did the Lord Christ, when he overcame evil with the power of love, and restored mankind, if they would, to their proper place. . .'

There was silence again. But before Hrethla had thought this out, she jumped up.

'Do you hear that?' There's a horn down the river. It's Uncle Renfrith!'

Renfrith it was, home from his long journey, and when they sat at dinner in the Big Hall that night, he told them all about it.

Oswald and his bodyguard had ridden far, far to the southern sea, to Dorcic (which we call Dorchester). There he had made a treaty with the king of the Gewissas (the men of Wessex, as we say), and had married his daughter, before travelling again to his own kingdom.

Renfrith had a present for every one of them. Hrethla's was a silver clasp for her belt, all the way from Frankland across the sea. But Renfrith kept Beren's present until last, and then he said to him, 'I have a message for you, which my Lord Oswald gave me when we parted: "Tell Beren Brightfingers to come to me now. He has minded your homestead for you long enough, and now he must come and be Steward of my stables, as I promised him once."'

Beren looked steadily at Renfrith.

'I had hoped for such a call from Bebbanburgh, my friend. But now it comes, I want to ask a further gift from you.'

'What then?'

'Something very valuable, from your house.'

In this way, Beren asked Renfrith, Wictred's son, for the hand of Ebba his sister in marriage. When the corn was gathered in, at the harvest supper, they were pledged together as man and wife as surely as might be.

'At Bebbanburgh,' said Beren, 'Aidan shall ask a Christian blessing on the marriage.'

Hrethla was to go with them. 'We want her to have a father and a mother,' said Beren. She quite agreed with this plan herself, but Lady Aldswith did not.

'What a life is mine! My son comes home at last, and he's full of mad, new ideas! My daughter leaves me to manage on my own, after all I've been through. And now you'll take the child, the only person who really understands how I feel and gives me some comfort.'

Hrethla was surprised at her grandmother's view of her.

'I'll stay, mama,' she told Ebba, as Lady Aldswith went on and on, 'if it makes it easier for her.'

So Hrethla stayed at Hundfelth, but it was understood

that one day they would come back and fetch her.

From harvest-time to Bloodmonth (November, we call it) when they did the winter slaughtering, Renfrith ran the farm and Lady Aldswith ran the house. Sibald married his girl, Hrosli, and brought her home to his cottage. Mildred, Thurstan's wife, had a baby. Hrethla ran about, helping in the kitchen and dairy when she could, working at the big looms as well as she was able, to make up for Ebba not being there, and going out on the moor alone, when nobody seemed to need her. She could not see that she was any comfort at all to Lady Aldswith, who took little enough notice of her, and she did not see at first that the scoldings Ebba used to have were now falling upon Freagifu.

In the middle of the pig-killing, the storm broke. Renfrith was cutting up an animal, Orca was salting, and in the kitchen, Lady Aldswith could be heard shouting, and Freagifu answering shrilly. Suddenly Freagifu ran out.

'I'll stay here no longer to be insulted. Renfrith Wictred's son, I'm going home now!'

Renfrith stood up, wiping his hands on his trousers. Lady Aldswith stood in the doorway.

'There you are, there you are, my fine son,' she raged. 'You and that good-for-nothing girl of yours, and murder unavenged between the two of you.'

Renfrith froze. 'I told you what I would do if this came up again. Listen,' he said to Freagifu, 'you are not going home. You are coming with me, to Bebbanburgh.'

And despite the work on hand, despite the time of year, despite Orca's appeals for common sense, Renfrith had taken his wife from the house before the day was out, on the first stage of the journey to the court of King Oswald.

12 A Strange Night

'Lady Frig is plucking her geese,' said Hrethla, as the first snowflakes came fluttering out of the sky. It was what Orca would have said if she had been there.

Since Renfrith had ridden away with Freagifu, Hundfelth had been dreary. The days ground by, each shorter than the last. The nights had yawned out, each swallowing more of the day than the one before. They celebrated Midwinter, just in the way Lady Aldswith wanted. After the Feast, the weather grew steadily colder, with a leaden hopelessness that matched all their feelings. The men finished the threshing and stopped coming up to the house. Even Wig often slept down at the cottages near his new sheepfold. There had been more bustle about the farmyard in the days before King Edwin fell, and then Lady Aldswith had brightened her grumbles by telling them how much better it would be when her dear son Renfrith came home.

On the morning of the day when the snow began, Orca had been called away to see a woman who was sick at Wulfings'. Snibba went with her, glad of a walk. A little later, Hrosli had come up from the cottages to ask Orca to come about Mildred's baby's croup. Surprising Hrethla, Gil had gone off to help, taking most of her rugs and blankets; she said Mildred had not enough. Hrethla was alone, except for Lady Aldswith, spinning in the weaving hall.

Hrethla made up the kitchen fire and stirred the stew in the pot. She milked the cows and fed them, and fetched in their water from the snowy yard. She let Fen out into the dark. He had grown savage with age and the recent changes. She dragged the gate to, and her chilled hands fumbled with the snow-clogged bolts.

Light shone across the yard behind her. Lady Aldswith had come out, to tell her to make haste.

There was a thump in the snowy quietness.

'Child! Hrethla!'

Lying in a heap by the weaving hall door, Lady Aldswith groaned. Hrethla left the gate still unbarred, and went to try to pull her up

'No. Leg's broken. Get me inside.'

By rolling and pulling they somehow brought her under cover.

'Quick, child, the fire.'

Hrethla looked round. Across the yard, the kitchen fire was flaring up. She ran to damp it down, terrified of a spark flying out and the whole place catching fire. It could happen so easily, she had often been told.

She took a long time making sure it was safe, and the stew went off the boil. When at last she came back to Lady Aldswith, there was little she could do to make her more comfortable. She let Hrethla bring her a pillow and a couple of blankets, but could not eat the stew with which Hrethla tried to feed her. When Hrethla wanted to do something about the broken leg, she said, 'No. Only make matters worse. Wait till Orca comes back.'

Hrethla sat on the floor beside her in the dim firelight. Everything had gone wrong, every happy thing that had happened since Uncle Renfrith came back was over. Everything was hopeless and lonely.

'Anybody there?'

Hrethla froze. There were footsteps in the snow. The door swung open. A shadowy figure blocked the sight of the falling snow.

'We come as friends. Peace – peace be to you.'

Hrethla sat stock still. The shadowy man came in, and another behind him, who said: 'What is it? Can we help?'

The Engle speech was better, but the voice was the same.

'You are Aidan the king's priest,' said Hrethla.

'Yes; how did you know?'

'You were at Hagulstad at Midsummer.'

'Are you ill, mother?'

Hrethla cut short her angry retort.

'My grandmother has broken her leg.'

'And you are all alone. Trumhere, we can be some use here.'

The young man came forward. He stirred the fire to give more light.

Aidan knew what to do, and Lady Aldswith had to let him do it. He sent Hrethla for bandages and bedding, he found a broomstick to which he tied the broken leg; with the young man, Trumhere, he moved the old lady onto the table top, and together they lifted it out of the draught, resting it on two of the boxes. Hrethla remembered that she ought to offer them some food. The stew had gone cold but Aidan heated what she brought over the weaving hall fire. Having no table did not bother him. They ate sitting on the floor as if they were out on the moor on a hunting trip, and when they had finished, Aidan said, 'Go to bed, my daughter. I will stay up and watch with your grandmother.'

Hrethla shook her head. She picked up her wolfskin, which had proved too heavy for Lady Aldswith's leg, wrapped herself in it and sat against the box like a dog on guard. Aidan was as still as any wild creature on the moor, but Trumhere shifted restlessly where he sat.

Lady Aldswith was not at ease either. She had groaned and cursed when Aidan set her leg and changed the furniture about, and when he asked a blessing on the food she muttered furiously, 'Woden confound the man.' She lay looking balefully at the helpful intruders.

'My son,' said Aidan, gently, 'let me hear you meditate upon the Scriptures.'

Trumhere said something in Scots.

'No,' said Aidan. 'Use the Engle, for I am still learning to speak the things of my Lord Jesus in that tongue.'

Trumhere sat looking into the fire for a minute and then began.

'Two trees there were in Paradise, the garden where God first set Man and his Wife to till it and to tend it. Of the first tree we know that from it they ate the fruit that was banned to them, and so fell into wrong and lost their happiness.

'But what of the second tree? For that was the Tree of Life, lost to Man and his Wife, but always they seek it while their earthly life lasts, and do not know how they can find it.

'So we find in the Psalms, in the first of the songs of Israel, the ancient people of God, that a man is called happy who delights in the law of God, and who meditates day and night upon his orderings. Such a man is like a tree planted beside the river, fruitful and never losing its leaves in the winter; and everything he does turns out right.

'Now what can that tree be, that the man is compared to, but the Tree of Life, with its roots set deep where water wells, and its fruit the nourishment of all living things, and its foliage unfailing.'

'Oh,' thought Hrethla, 'now he is talking about something I know,' and while she sat still as a dog on duty, her mind grew sharp and bright as Trumhere continued to speak slowly, with pauses when he was stuck, to see what he would say about the Tree of Life.

'And who is that man who delights in God's law and loves its orderings? For this is what many a man may wish to do but cannot command himself to do it. In all the days of Middle Earth there has never been a man but one who was like that.

'And this was the Man Christ Jesus. Lord of Heaven and Earth, He came to be a Man amongst men, and his joy was to know and to do everything as God had commanded it. Lovelier Lord there has never been known to the companions he chose. To the people he gave great bounty, but not of gold rings. For his was the power of God, and he gave health to the sick, and sight to the blind, speech to the dumb and strength to the cripples unable to walk. Not only so, but in words he showed to all the heart of God, and his speech was sweeter than honey.

'Yet what came of this upon the earth? The envy of the priests of that nation caused him to be given up to the Romans. The tree that was prepared for him was no Tree of Life, but the cross of wood on which the Romans stretched a man to suffer death. So he died as men died who were rebels under the Roman rule.

'No Tree of Life that cross appeared to be, but the tree of a curse, and yet it became the greatest joy and comfort to mankind. For what they could not know, who did the Lord Christ to death, was that this too was the purpose of God. Only if he embraced death could he penetrate the enemy's stronghold, the place of death, and win a way of release for man from the exile and loss. In that battle the Lord Christ was victor, but he gave a greater ransom than any king has ever given for the freedom of his dear friends; he gave his life most precious. Three days he was held in death, and on the third he rose again to life.

'His friends saw him again, all those who had been his companions before that time of sorrow, his Mother, and the women who had served him. For forty days he went about on Middle Earth again, and after that he ascended into Heaven, the bright land from which he had come, to which he will lead at last all his faithful warriors.

'And what do we know of that country of joy to which he calls us? In the book of the blessed John is written the song of that city all of gold. A river flows through it clear as crystal, the water of life, and beside the river on either bank, trees bearing the best of fruits, whose leaves heal all the quarrels of the peoples.

'But that city is the city of the Lord Christ and God for ever and ever; it is full of his presence, and the Tree of Life that grows beside the water is itself a picture of him who died on the Tree and lives, to bring all who hold to him out of misery into freedom, into life, into the joy of God, into delight in knowing him.'

So went Trumhere's meditation on the far side of the fire, while Hrethla watched the listening smile on Aidan's face, and saw the trees of the golden city in the golden embers, and Lady Aldswith slept fitfully and groaned.

Then suddenly, it was morning, with the white light from the snow cast up against the roof beams from the open door, and Trumhere curled on the floor, asleep, and Aidan rebuilding the fire. He saw Hrethla looking, and nodded reassuringly towards Lady Aldswith.

Hrethla moved nearer the fire.

'Where are the rest of the people?' Aidan questioned quietly.

'They've – all gone away.'

'Who is the headman of the settlement?'

'Renfrith Wictred's son.'

'Oh. Him they call Sharpshooter?'

'Yes. Of course, you know him. My uncle.'

'Oh?' Aidan looked towards the makeshift bed.

'Yes, Lady Aldswith's his mother.'

'I see. And your name is . . .?'

'Hrethla Ingui's daughter.'

'And where are the rest of the people?'

'Down at the cottages. They'll be coming up. At least they will if I fetch Fen in. He's our watchdog. I don't know, really, how you missed him last night, unless you put a spell on him.'

'No. I pray, I don't make spells.' Aidan was making scones to griddle on the fire.

'I thought so. How did you find this place?'

'We lost ourselves in the snow. We had visited a settlement on the other side of the river, and should have gone back to Hagulstad. We knew we were badly out of our way, and when we saw a bright light we made for it. Then it disappeared. I think we met your Fen, however. A huge grey dog with a slavering muzzle? He came out of the snow and fog and led us up here to the gate: it was open, so we thought something was wrong.'

Hrethla stood up, took off the wolfskin and put on her cape. She went to the kitchen to find some meat and bones. She thought the king's priest was clever to come and forage out the barley flour in a strange place.

She went to the gate and called. Fen came, ferocious as usual, and she barely managed to put down his food in the place where she could chain him as he crunched and worried at the chunk of old sheep.

She went outside, and stood by the ash tree, looking down the track.

In later years, when there was great talk of miracles attaching to the king and Aidan, Hrethla told people about Fen's behaviour at that time. Nobody would have it that there was anything extraordinary about it. 'Oh well, animals have this sense. He knew it was a holy man, and would do no harm. And you were a child, too much afraid of the dog.'

But Hrethla knew, then and later, that she was no more afraid than need be, and that with Fen as he was then, it took nothing less than the power of the Lord Christ for him to have led the strangers to the homestead.

She stood with her hand on the ash tree, looking at the blown snow on the ground, and the black and white branches below. The clouds that had weighed down the sky for days were gone, leaving a sky of milky white and thin blue.

Everything was all of a sudden very real. Real as the ash tree by the gate was the cross of wood on which the Lord Christ died in the days of the Romans, who had built the Wall across the moor. Real as the tree that carried all life in its branches was the escape way that the boldest of Warriors had made out of the place of misery and death into the happiness of living and the heart of God. Real as Snibba's trust in Hrethla, and all the bonds of family and lordship that made sense of the lives of everyone she knew, there sprang in her then such loyalty to Christ Jesus as made him her Lord for life.

Then Gil came up the field path.

13 Full Payment

For three weeks Lady Aldswith lay flat on the table top, keeping her leg still and her tongue sharp on anyone who tried to make anything comfortable for her, usually Orca. Thurstan came up and worked around the farmstead every day and Wig and Duffa were certain to sleep there each night. Snow melted, the wind blew mild, and the days lengthened. One morning they heard Renfrith's horn by the river. Freagifu was with him.

'Renfrith Wictred's son, what do you think you are up to, dragging that poor girl round the countryside at this time of day?' Orca scolded, but she was pleased to see him, and Freagifu looked very pleased with herself.

Lady Aldswith was not at all welcoming. She glowered at her son.

'So you've come back. Well, don't take in hand to bury me, like these Christmen do. I want a good burning, like our people have always had.'

'But Mother!' Renfrith was taken aback. 'Who said you were going to die?'

'I did,' snapped Lady Aldswith. 'I'll only clutter up the place, with a game leg.'

Renfrith did not explain what had made him come home, but Orca had her ideas. 'Aidan had a hand in that,' she said. 'He came to Wulfings from here, and made sure I knew where I was needed.'

Later on, just as a sharp frosty spell broke the incoming spring, Beren and Ebba came riding home. Elfric Wulfing was with them, and the three men began an immediate consultation, while Ebba went straight in to see her mother.

This left Hrethla with Ban. She put her arms round him and rested her head on his shoulder.

'What's it like at Bebbanburgh, Ban?' she asked him. 'Are the king's horses beautiful? And does my Mama like it with all the great ladies at the court?'

She had the answer to that from Beren, a little later on.

'She doesn't like it there at all,' he told Hrethla. 'There's no work for her, and she feels quite lost. But the king has given me a farm, and as soon as I have the houses put to rights, I shall come back and fetch you both to live there. I must go back to the king's stables. I'm only staying this one night.'

But Beren stayed longer than one night.

Hrethla had looked forward to being with her mother at bedtime but Ebba put her off.

'I shall sit up to-night. Orca's tired, and Grandmother's got a nasty little cough. I want you to sleep down at Hrosli's.'

So Hrethla spent the night at the cottage; and Lady Aldswith died in the night.

'And now what do we do?' demanded Renfrith.

They were standing in the weaving hall by the ashes of the fire, and the question was what to do about the funeral, Christian burial or heathen burning.

'You'll do as she said,' answered Orca.

Renfrith looked at Beren. Beren just stood still, with his arm round Ebba's shoulders, and Hrethla, on the other side, stood still hoping not to be noticed.

'What else can you do?' Elfric settled it.

'You'll need her boxes over here,' said Orca.

'That's one.' Ebba was more alive to what was needed than they thought. 'And that. The other's nothing but bedcoverings.'

They pulled Lady Aldswith's huge wooden chest out from the shadowy bedroom end of the hall. It had no lock or key. No one would have dreamt of looking in it but the mistress of the house until now. Ebba raised the lid. On the top lay Lady Aldswith's finest dress and underdress. Ebba took this out and laid it aside.

Underneath were all the clothes Lady Aldswith had ever worn, even to some her boys had had when young. Ebba picked out a fine cloak, a headscarf of the best linen, and shoes.

'Now the smaller box,' she said, and knelt to the job. She folded back the cloak on top. 'What about that?'

A collar of gold lay there, shaped like an exaggerated moon crescent, to be worn on the front of a garment. Renfrith considered.

'Yes.'

Hrethla, standing numb and stupid, realized that all this was to decide what Lady Aldswith should wear to the Halls of the Dead, whose touch was already upon her, and she suddenly wanted to scream. But she stood as still as before, and noticed that the men were much more interested in this box than in the first one.

There was a necklet to go with the collar, of linked gold plates. Several other necklets, lighter and prettier, Ebba left. There were bundles of copper armbands, a belt of gold wire and coloured stones, and several massive cloak brooches.

'Rings,' prompted Orca.

'You don't see things like this now,' murmured Ebba.

'Who'd have thought the lady had all this?' Elfric marvelled softly.

'There are things here I've never seen,' Renfrith muttered to him.

Beren kept his prudent silence, but none of them questioned that the best and showiest of the treasures should be heaped upon the lady at her funeral.

Ebba had found the finger rings, rolled up in a cloth. She spread it out and the rings tumbled across it, plain gold, patterned, or set with bulky stones. Renfrith peered, considering. Hrethla indicated with her finger a further bundle, rolled together. Ebba, obedient to Renfrith's nod, undid it.

It was a cluster of plain gold rings, held together with a leather thong. Money, as Hrethla knew, but she was not prepared for the frozen silence which fell upon the grown-ups.

Ebba looked up helplessly.

Deliberately, Beren took the bunch and counted the rings in plain view of them all.

'Compensation,' breathed Orca.

'The value of a fighting man's life,' concluded Beren.

'Redpath.' Ebba's word was a sigh.

'So she had it all the time. Then why deny it?' said Renfrith holding his head.

'But –.' Elfric was about to burst out. Beren gave him a look as much as to say, 'Not here.' They went on sorting through the rings, picking out seven to put with the clothing; shoe buckles, head rail, pendants for the belt; Renfrith and Ebba chose the best of every dress ornament to honour their mother. At last the chests were closed. Renfrith took Hrethla's hand and they went out into the yard, leaving Ebba and Orca in the weaving hall.

'I must go,' said Elfric.

'You must have something to eat first. Go along, Snippet, see what you can find in the kitchen,' Renfrith suggested.

Hrethla found some sad old scones and a piece of bacon with just a slice off, and took these, with some butter and some ale, into the Hall. The tables were not up, so she put them down on the benches by the men and poured for them. Elfric broke the heavy silence.

'It's a bad time of year for meat.'

'We'll manage.' Renfrith hesitated. 'Will your people come over? Will you ask them to come?'

'You can.'

'Yes,' said Renfrith. 'I'll see to it.'

'Why did she hide it?' said Elfric.

'She wanted a vengeance of blood,' said Beren. 'The good old-fashioned way, with one killing leading to another.'

'She never would admit that it had been settled legally,' said Renfrith.

'But you didn't believe her?'

'No.'

'Well, you asked no end of questions. It was hard on my uncle.'

'What you don't know,' said Beren, 'is how hard it was on Renfrith here. How did you keep cool, Sharpshooter, under her insults?'

Renfrith looked down the horn at his ale.

'I didn't,' he said at last. 'She made it seem as if I were not a man if I didn't do what she wanted. And although I had your friendship and Freagifu to think of, and I wanted to believe that your uncle had put things straight, I think I should have taken it up as a blood feud if it had not been – if I had not thought it would be – oh, unworthy of Christ's man.'

There was a thoughtful silence, during which the bacon went on disappearing, and then Elfric took his leave.

'Uncle Renfrith's braver than I knew,' thought Hrethla, clearing up the food.

So the Wulfings came to Hundfelth at last, for Lady Aldswith's funeral, all except Wulfwine, who they said, had gone to see about a horse and had not come back yet. As for Freagifu, she had kept out of Lady Aldswith's way when she was ill, and she did much the same now, staying down at Mildred's on the day of the funeral.

They let Hrethla see Lady Aldswith that morning, in all the finery of cloth and jewels many-coloured, her hard face white as candles in the midst of it all. Hrethla thought she must already have gone to the ice-halls in all but outward seeming, and wondered, vaguely, if the clothes would follow after. Then she knew for a minute most painfully, that she had lost her grandmother, who, harsh and miserable as she had always been, had kept the homestead going all through her own childhood. At that, the horn sounded in the woods, which meant that the Wulfings were coming, and she never recovered the moment of grief. Only, she knew that not just one person, but a whole epoch was going away with Aldswith.

They had built a huge bonfire on the ridge above the house, and they carried her and laid her on it. Elfric's father made a speech, which was really more about the early days of settling the land than about Lady Aldswith herself. The gold and gems gleamed above the well-stacked wood, and Hrethla, looking at it, thought with a shudder of all the rest, stored in the little chest.

'Never do I want such treasure,' she said to herself.

The fire came up readily; it was a good burning. Ebba wailed and sobbed, and could not stop herself, and when the sun was going down and they went back, Beren turned aside at the first room they came to, which was Orca's, and sat her down on the edge of the bed.

'It's all right, Mama. You've got me and you've got Beren,' Hrethla kept saying, feeling, as at other times, that it was all wrong, because Ebba was the mother and she was the little girl. Beren said nothing, but kept a firm hold on Ebba until she lay down, worn out. Orca came in.

'Oh, I'm glad you're here. Shall I stay?'

'No, you've done enough, Orca. Go and have dinner.

Only, if Ebba could stay here to-night with you when I'm in the Hall . . .'

'Yes, that's right. Better than in the weaving hall.' Orca went off to the Big Hall from which a good deal of noise could already be heard. Everybody was tired and hungry, and relieved that the funeral was over.

'Stay here, little daughter,' said Beren. 'I'll fetch you something to eat.'

Hrethla hardly thought to see him come back. Fighting men did not, in her experience, serve food to little girls, certainly not to save them going in to dinner with everybody else. But there he was, with food and drink, and the little Hall harp tucked under his arm. He roused Ebba, and Hrethla perched on the corner of Orca's box where the eatables had been put, handing things, and thinking how nice it was to eat sitting down with the grown-ups; and afterwards Beren played to them quietly on the harp.

14 A Time of Change

After this the spring farm work went forward steadily with Renfrith in charge. Beren went back to Bebbanburgh. Ebba worked hard with Orca, bringing the kitchen and dairy back into order. She was too busy to be unhappy, and soon they were busier still, for Freagifu had a baby boy. Everybody was delighted with him, and Hrethla thought it was wonderful to have a cousin of her own. Renfrith held a special dinner to celebrate, and no-one in the settlement stayed away from the Big Hall that night. It was Pasch (which we call Easter now), the time when the Lord Christ had the victory over his foes and rose up from the dead by the power of God. This Renfrith told them about when he said prayers in the Hall before dinner, and thanked God for it, but also for the safe coming of his son, and for Freagifu's health.

At first, Freagifu had all her time occupied with the baby, but as she began to take up her old jobs again, Ebba stood aside, waiting on her, giving her turns at new ones.

'You will be Lady here,' she seemed to say, but only in her manner. She never gave Hrethla orders, any more than she ever had done, and when they went to bed in the weaving hall, she simply went to sleep.

Hrethla was happy and busy all day long, with work that was not too heavy for her. There were plenty of young animals to look after, and it was wonderful how much extra water and firewood seemed to be needed for the baby, when you thought how small he was.

One evening, when the baby was going on for seven

weeks old, she came in from the fields to find Aidan of Hy talking to her uncle in the farmyard. He was travelling round the settlements preaching the word of Christ, as usual with one or two young men, but he had come to Hundfelth alone. Of course, Renfrith told him to stop the night. He sat in the guest seat at dinner, and when Hrethla poured the ale, he said, 'Thanks Hrethla Ingui's daughter. I am glad we meet again,' and Hrethla was glad he remembered her.

At the end of dinner, Renfrith announced that they would have prayers with their visitor. Everyone was quiet at once; they wanted to know what the king's priest would do.

Aidan stood and prayed in the Engle speech. He said the prayers that Renfrith used, but Aidan prayed as if he were talking directly to God. Everyone understood, and knew when it came to the places to say Amen, so they all said 'Amen' very fervently.

Then Aidan said, 'Hear, my friends. God, the living God, has spoken. He has called the earth, from farthest east to farthest west. Out of Zion, perfect in beauty, God has shone forth; from the stronghold of his ancient people, his light has come. He calls to the heavens to show his justice, and to the earth, to tell people who seek him that he has decreed. You have sacrificed animals, and brought cakes in honour of the gods, but he, the living God, will take no bullock from your house, nor ram from your fold.

'For every beast of the forest is his, and the cattle upon a thousand hills. He knows all the birds of the mountain, and all the roaming creatures of the moors belong to him. If he could be hungry, he would not tell us; the world is his and all its produce.

'What you can offer to God is thanksgiving; loyalty you can render to him high in heaven. Cry to him in trouble and he will rescue; then you will know how wonderful he is.

'But to the obstinate heathen, God says, "What do you

want with my orderings? Do not pretend to make a pact with me. You hate good teaching and throw out the words of the good news. You only want thieving and cheating, bad words and lying, bad faith between kinsmen and quarrels amongst relations. You have done all such things and I have not interfered, but now I tell you about them, and now is the time to put things right".

'Consider this, if you wish not to be bothered with God, lest he ruins your affairs, and you have no hope of rescue.

'The man who turns to praise God has learned what is true: if you change your way of life to please God you will see the salvation that he shows you in Christ the Lord.'

The people of Hundfelth would have applauded, but Aidan silenced them and finished with a short prayer. When he sat down they began talking, and Hrethla was just about to go round with the ale again when Renfrith turned from their guest and thumped the table for silence.

'Listen,' he said. 'You have heard the words of Aidan, the priest of Oswald the King. He says that he thought he must have come to a place of the Christmen, such good understanding you gave him. But I told him that there are none here who have received the grace of baptism, except myself. And he says, if there are any who wish it, let them prepare themselves so as to be baptised at Pentecost. Many from the places round about will join themselves to Christ then. But I say, let nobody pledge his faith carelessly, or just because I, who am lord here, am Christ's man.'

The Hall was completely still for a moment. Then Sibald jumped up.

'Christ is Lord,' he cried.

Excited talk broke out. All the men wanted to have their say. However much they approved of Renfrith's ways, not one of them meant to change without giving his views or asking some sharp questions. Ebba sent Hrethla to bed while the discussion was still very confused.

Aidan stayed at Hundfelth for two days, and in that time he had a talk with practically everybody about the place. Wig said he was too old for new ways and went off to the hills, but he said Duffa could do as he liked.

On the second evening, when Hrethla had curled up under her wolfskin, Ebba came and sat on the edge of the bed.

'What do you think about it, darling?' she said.

Hrethla knew exactly what she meant. She sat up.

'Oh, yes. Please. But what about you?'

Ebba looked at the floor.

'It's the right thing, I think,' she said. 'He is kind, this Christ. You see that he cared enough to die for the people. And not only the fighting men; you know that he cared about the women too, and their children. It is a great advantage having to do with just one God, that cares about the women and everybody, all the different countries too. I think that must surely be how it is.'

The next morning Hrethla found Orca in a quiet place.

'What do you think, Orca?'

Orca knew what she was driving at.

'Hum,' she said. 'Well, I can see there's more in this Christ-faith than meets the eye. And this Aidan, he's one of the right sort. Yes, I shall go in for it.'

Late in the afternoon, as the tables were being put up for dinner, Aidan said, 'Come here, Hrethla. When I was here before, you made me your guest, and now you have not a word to say to me.'

He sat down on one of the Hall benches, and Hrethla stood in front of him.

'You were busy with the older people. But, truthfully, I am very grateful that you came that other time.'

'Well, I can tell you we were glad to find ourselves under cover. But now tell me something: what do you think of the Lord Christ?'

'He is my Lord for life.'

'I see. So you will be coming to the river this Sunday, at Pentecost, to pledge him your life?'

'Yes.'

'But do you know that means leaving all the old life behind? And forgetting about the gods of which your grandmother taught you?'

'It's all right. There was only trouble. And they're gone, anyway.'

Aidan looked at her hard, to see if she meant it. 'Do you understand that the Lord Christ laid down his life for you so that your life should be made new in him?'

'Yes,' said Hrethla.

Aidan said some more, and then told her to kneel down. He put his hands on her head and prayed for the blessing of God to be on her. When she stood up, he said, 'And now I will tell you something. Beren Brightfingers is coming in time for the baptising, and afterwards he will take you and your mother back with him.'

It was time for dinner, and the end of the conversation. She thought, afterwards, that Aidan was not sure she understood properly. But it seemed quite simple to her, and she wished she could tell him so for certain. However, he left early next day, Renfrith walking with him as far as the ford.

By the middle of the morning, Hrethla could not bear feeling excited any more. She took her bow and arrows and went out on the moor with Snibba. She walked fast, springing through the heather on bare feet, running and jumping, full of joy, like a fighting man going to meet his own lord for some great adventure. All at once, she found she was full of sadness at the same time.

Everything was changing, too fast to keep up with it. She must leave the moor, and the farmstead she knew, and who could tell what would befall at Bebbanburgh? Would

Mama be the same? And Beren, would he be the kind friend he had always been? What was it like, living near the king, among Christmen all the time? Would she do it right?

The tears were wet on her face as she stumbled down the slope and came upon the burn. The sheep path failed. She hitched up her skirts and walked up the stream bed until her feet were numb. Then there was grass to come out on to, and she followed the bank until she came to the Meres. She stood under the alder trees, between the banks of rushes, and now her heart was aching for her father, that unknown man with the sword boar-crested, who might have been Beren's foster-brother. Caught in the struggle between the kings, he had ended his life as a serving man and steward, saving the sheep on a farm that was not his own. Here was the water where he had struggled one winter night; on the far side were the hills where he had hunted for food and killed the big wolf. She had always meant to go to those hills one day with Wig, and now there was no more time.

She remembered that her father had given her a name of hope. 'Spring will come again,' he said.

Regardless of the conflict between Ida's line and Alla's son, spreading healing over the wrongs that had come of it, springing like a new branch of a great tree, the new life of the Lord Christ had come to the land. Of that Tree she was part; happiness and hope were hers in it too. Though the old gods were gone, the Tree was not lost in which all life was nourished, all longing satisfied. It was only changed; in that change was nothing to fear. The Lord Christ had done it, whose death was fearless; the life that sprang from it knew no source of disaster. Its roots reached deep in the regions of time, its high boughs penetrated the presence of the Living God; to be in those branches was better than any safety.

It was as if the Lord Christ had come to meet her on the

moor and tell her so, and she said to him; 'Thank you for coming. Thank you for letting me get to know you on my own piece of moor. And I don't need to worry about Ingui and all the people in olden times. You'll have seen to it all. And it's bound to be all right at Bebbanburgh.'

She skirted the Meres and climbed the broken cliffs to the Wall. She made her way back along it, watching the distant hills, and talking to the Lord Christ. The wind was rough, her hair came undone, and her bow jolted at her back. Even Snibba was tired, and padded close at her side, brushing her bare legs. Late in the afternoon she came within sight of home.

Someone was waiting for her on the ridge, a man with a big dog. It was Beren with Ban, of course. Ban came forward to put his nose in her hand, but Beren stood still until she came, and he kissed her forehead.

'Good health, Hrethla Ingui's daughter. Do you know that you are very like him? My foster brother, I mean. I never saw it before.'

'Am I?' said Hrethla. 'I'm glad.'

They went in to dinner together.

15 All Things New

In the meadow by the river was a great crowd, more than a hundred people together, as Hrethla heard tell later, and Aidan stood above them on the slope and addressed them in the Engle tongue.

He spoke of the fair day on which they were gathered there, and how it should be the beginning of days, a new birthday, for many of them that stood there and were about to be washed in the waters of baptism. Then he warned them that they must be sure to repent of all evil and all wrong-doing that they had done in the past; and he asked if they would turn right away from their former gods to the true and living God their Saviour. He called on all those who were coming for baptism to stand forward and to them he put these questions and they all answered together.

Now Aidan, Oswald's priest, stood in the shallows, and one by one, family after family, his companions called on those who should come forward. They went into the water to Aidan, in new white wool tunics, and he dipped them under, and spoke the holy words. When it came to Hrethla's turn she loosed Orca's hand and stepped down the bank. Then there was Aidan's voice coming over her head, and the water . . . and she stood up with a splutter, dripping; herself, Hrethla, baptised in the Name of the Father and of the Son, and of the Holy Spirit, Christ's man for good and all in the sight of everybody. Someone helped her up the bank and out of the wind, chill on her soaking shift, to the shelter rigged up in the bushes. When she came out, dressed and dry, she stood where the sun tempered the breeze, and watched, while Aidan went on baptising and baptising.

It was done. And now Beren and Renfrith, and the young men with Aidan, had put tables out in the flattest part of the meadow, and they all gathered round, standing like children to eat, men at one table and women at another. Up from the water, Aidan blessed the food, and the bread and cheese and honey and ale that was on those tables seemed the best food Hrethla had ever tasted.

Then Aidan was speaking, with his venerable beard and radiant face, as before; speaking of souls washed clean and of life in Christ, of time to come, earthly temptation and heavenly joys, and praying, as Aidan prayed, straight to God.

So he dismissed the company and they turned to go to their homes, walking back by the way they had come, some along the South River to the west, some to Hagulstad, while the people from Hundfelth, with some from the Wulfings and other settlements, set off up the North River towards the ford beside the Wall.

When they had come in the early morning, one group after another joining together, they had sung and praised God as they went, to keep the pace up. Now they were quiet, or went with murmuring voices. To Hrethla, walking beside Ebba and Beren, it seemed as if the singing of the morning still hung upon the air around her. She could see the people streaming on in front, she could feel the people walking behind her; and their long shadows, all together, moved across the grass on her right. 'So many people,' she thought, from the middle of tiredness, 'and all of them covered by the Tree that the Lord Christ died on.' In her head she saw it at the front of the procession, towering, stark and bare. But then it was not bare, it was full of leaves and fruits and life, and they were all being drawn into it, all the people. They were all part of the Tree together, and there, going on in front, was the Lord Christ. So thought Hrethla as she went through the long twilight, home to Hundfelth for the last time, and the new life beyond.